"*The Prodigy* is Norman Weissman's hilarious portrayal of a young runaway whose sojourn across America pits youthful innocence against the vagaries of people, regions and beliefs in a bygone era before the Second World War. This is an allegory. A secular Pilgrim's Progress that pays subtle homage to Mark Twain and John Steinbeck and reveals unexpected truths from encounters with improbable characters and events that will keep you guessing about who is being parodied. *The Prodigy* traverses a landscape reflecting the generosity and greed, openness and prejudice, love and hatred that defines the richness of our American experience."

Larry Dowler
Archivist, Yale University
(1970-1982)
Librarian, Widener Library, Harvard University
(1982-1998)

"An amazing book. An amazing story. Reading *The Prodigy* I hear your voice and see the sweep of a huge portion of American history. If I had to find words to describe this work I'd call it a quintessentially American story with all the genius, freedom and creativity as well as all the perversity the word implies. Your narrator paints vivid pictures of pre-World War II America where not all dreams come true."

Forrest Stone MFA, Playwright, Teacher,
Yale School of Drama
Author : *No sign After This Sign*

"Norman Weissman has done it again. His near photographic memory allows him to recall the history of most of the previous century. His humanity embraces the striving and suffering of the masses. His artistry creates a picaresque novel of insight, adventure and comedy. His hero confronts a parade of iconic characters. His fantastical plots, heart breaking and hilarious, sweep the reader along from one escapade to another."

Norman Thomas Marshall
Co-Author *John Brown, Trumpet of Freedom*
Gwen Gunn
Nationally published Poet and Founder, The Westbeth Playwrights Feminist Collective.

"Norman Weissman is a superb writer and storyteller. His latest book *The Prodigy* is a series of interrelated vignettes. It uniquely captures the lives of Americans during the Great Depression. In addition to his storytelling talent he makes the reader suffer through his character's travails. Weissman's intense feeling for American History makes this book a remarkable reading experience."

Herman J. Obermeyer, Author
Soldiering For Freedom: A G.I.s account of World War II and *Rehnquist,* a personal portrait of the distinguished Chief Justice of the United States.

THE PRODIGY

A Novel

By
Norman Weissman

Published in The United States of America by
Hammonasset House Books, Mystic CT
Cataloging-in-Publication Data available from
Library of Congress
History / Fiction ISBN 978-0-9966169-0-4

FICO: 14000

www.HammonassetHouse.com

Cover design: Lee A. Jacobus

Printed in the United States of America

In loving memory of:
Bernard Weissman
(1921-1946)

The greatest thing a human soul ever does in this world is to see something and tell what it saw in a plain way... To see clearly is poetry and religion all in one.

John Ruskin (1819-1900)

ONE

In 1934 when dance marathons and flag pole sitting diverted attention from the anxieties of the Great Depression, a fifteen year old boy wearing a backpack and sun hat roller skating along US-6 appeared to be just another destitute wanderer sleeping in barns, haystacks and roadside campsites. A vagabond roaming our land looking for work and a better future.

Years later, in 1980, when Emiliano Dante was living in Brooklyn and commuting to Manhattan he saw that boy, now an old man, standing under the stairs of a subway station where the tracks ran elevated above the street.

He was now a street musician playing the violin for nickels, dimes and quarters dropped into the violin case at his feet. Winter or summer, rain or shine, he performed for commuters who stopped to hear such popular favorites as *Jeannie With The Light Brown Hair, None But The Lonely Heart* and *Flight of The Bumblebee*. Every afternoon, before the evening rush hour provided a new audience, he left the station to play in apartment courtyards where lonely housewives leaned out their windows to applaud and occasionally throw down coins.

He seemed heroic and tragic, a musician surviving hard times. Dante complimented his performance. He nodded a thank you and asked the name of his favorite composer.

"Chopin," Dante replied. The Old Man smiled approval of his choice playing Chopin's Nocturne in E-Flat major with passion and beauty. Impressed by his performance Dante asked his name. "Yiddle mit de Fiddle," he said, in Yiddish, smiling, shaking his head. Joking. "Yiddle mit de fiddle," he repeated before resuming his usual repertoire. Dante laughed, walked on thinking his playing will vanish with the night. Here today, gone tomorrow. There but for the grace of God go I.

"You know who he is?" asked a short well-dressed man, another commuter who appreciated his playing. "He was once famous," he explained, shaking his head for emphasis. "A child prodigy," he said. "A celebrity. I think his name was Berl."

To satisfy his curiosity Dante went to the main New York Public Library where he had time to read and think trying to answer a now compelling question – who was this old man expressing the sorrows of life with such feeling? Searching the music archives with a first name as a lead, intimidated by a quagmire of newspaper clippings, interviews, and concert reviews, Dante was overwhelmed by possibilities. Each new clue brought other possibilities in view. Dante became obsessed. Berl was a Russian name. Or was it also English? Certainly not American. And he wondered what was the life of a young violinist named Berl like? A child prodigy who loved applause as he fingered the strings of his violin in the ecstasy of creation, a virtuoso responding to audiences with encores that evoked feelings of sadness, pathos and beauty. With hair flowing down to his shoulders, with baby fat vanishing as he grew older, he wore short black velvet pants, knee high-stockings and a white silk shirt sustaining his image of a child prodigy touring the world performing more than thirty concerts a year.

Schooled at home, with companionship restricted to family, Berl found his tutoring, study and practice hours failed to subdue his youthful spirit, his feeling that there must be more to life than sacrificing his childhood making music. He had physical strength he wanted to use beyond home and concert halls. Prohibited from contact sports, a discipline imposed by his parents, he defied their disapproval and bought a pair of roller skates. With wings attached to his shoes, soaring over the pavement, heart pounding against the walls of his chest, he enjoyed freedom's fresh air, a welcome break from practicing six hours a day, lonely and isolated in a small room. Skating Brooklyn's streets and avenues, Berl discovered the infinite variety of humanity, where rich and poor, black and white, immigrants and native born lived and worked, struggling to fulfill dreams of prosperity and happiness. Skating to the bay near his home, his lungs filled with the tang of fresh salt air, Berl watched battered fishing boats bring in their daily catch unloaded by heroic fishermen who defied storms to feed their families. Berl saw the beauty and wonder and tragedy of life when the fishermen told him that mournful seagull cries were the souls of men lost at sea, a soul-stirring thought for a precocious boy who struggled to become a man awake to opportunities his parents denied him. When he fell and broke his arm while skating, confined to his room until the bones healed, Berl wondered if he could ever return to the rigid discipline he once accepted as normal. Berl recognized what was happening to him. He felt the pain and frustration of being used to satisfy his parents' ambitions. That insight brought tears to Dante's eyes. He felt like an intruder watching a boy yearning for a better life.

Wearing long hair, velvet shorts, and knee-high stockings humiliated him. He wanted to be part of a world where boys wore long pants, sweatshirts, and baseball caps. He wanted to stop travelling as a celebrity and become ordinary, an impossible dream he never shared with his parents. And so Berl ran away from home.

Disappeared. Became a missing person whose playing now survived on 12 inch 78-RPM recordings selling for six figures when auctioned. Berl became history revered by music critics who mourned the disappearance of a great violinist.

Dante learned Berl's life was shaped by a child's limited knowledge of the world. Fleeing a cloistered existence, unaware of what he did not know, his adventures, trials, and tribulations taught Berl accepting pain was a condition of living. He determined when his youth was gone he would never look back upon his life with sorrow and the regret of knowing he once had a passion for living and wasted its possibilities. He did not want to look back and remember he once had strength enough for every challenge and never used it.

And so through the chill of wind and rain, Berl skated across New Jersey and Pennsylvania and over the Appalachian Hills into Ohio's and Indiana's prairie farmlands. Sleeping in barns, haystacks, and roadside campsites, with the stars as companions, Berl learned to read the music of the heavens. The Constellations. The Bear. The Hunter and The Big Dipper became friends he looked at every night realizing it was possible to choose his destiny.

With little knowledge of the world and its ways, the comedy and tragedy of Berl's life was inevitable. Roller skating across America Berl read his book of memories, chapters of joy and sorrow preserving his past. For to forget is to abort a consciousness that can only be restored by embracing the world like a lover, keeping memories alive, discovering the true profession of Man is to find his way to himself. For when we begin to see we are challenged to see more not less. To strive, to seek, to find and not to yield is Life's true glory.

One morning a battered pick-up entered the campsite where Berl had been sleeping intruding upon his solitude with silence-shattering Gospel music. The driver, tall, unshaven, wearing bib overalls stepped out of the truck and walked to him shouting: "Are you the damned fool roller skater I almost run over yesterday?" Recalling the incident Berl hesitated before nodding yes. The driver, glaring at him asked: "Where in hell do you think you are going?" Berl turned and walked away. Frightened. Refusing to talk. "You must be going somewhere," the driver called out. Berl stopped, turned and faced his inquisitor.

"California," he replied. "California."

"California!" the driver shouted. "California? That's just about the stupidest idea I've ever heard of. Only a damn fool would go roller skating all the way to California." The driver looked around the campsite as if searching for someone. "You all by yourself?" he asked. Then turning to Berl he said, "Come to think of it I'm going to California myself." He paused. Friendly. Smiling, asking: "How bout you ride with me?"

Surprised, Berl remained silent. Considered the invitation.

"Didn't your mother ever tell you not to play in the street?" the driver said in the voice of a Gospel Preacher admonishing a congregation.

Berl laughed, thought about it, and without hesitation accepted the invitation. "Yes thanks, I'll ride with you," he replied.

The driver raised his arms as if praising God shouting: "Great God Almighty these highways are built for murder. Nothing but crazy lazy drivers. Drunk or sober. Believe me they'd run you down for sure and leave nothing but Road Kill. Better you ride with me if you want to live." He spat a dark stream of tobacco juice. With the back of his hand he wiped his mouth. Pounding his fist into his palm he shouted: "What this world is coming to ain't nice I tell you. Ain't no good at all. Nothing but killing and rape and thievery and fornication with man woman and beast. And there's no end of these abominations, I tell you. No end at all. What the world is coming to is a living Hell. You can take my word for it. A living Hell!"

Berl listened, remained silent, turning to look at the beauty of an Indiana Spring. Trees ending their winter sleep, the countryside turning from brown to green. Scenery he now appreciated. A bird singing in a nearby tree at sunrise.

The driver looked up. Listening to the song. His eyes filled with the wonder of the moment. Then with religious fervor, possessed, he shouted: "Praised be his holy name! I'm a lover of the Lord! God is his Father! Jesus is me brother! Mary is his mother! Baptized in the blood of the Lamb! Oh yes! Yes! I'm a lover of the Lord! That's who I am. Take my word for it." Suddenly calm. Thoughtful. Curious. He turned and looked at Berl. "What's your name," he asked.

"Berl."

The driver shook his head. "What kind of name is that?"

"I don't know." Berl replied.

"Great God Almighty," the driver said. "Names is important. Jake's my name. Someone who's been to Hell and back and lived to tell about it. You can call me Jake. That's me all right. Bin to Hell and back again. Know everything there is to know about Hell. 'bout violence and lies and treachery an greed and heresy. Yes siree Bob if you ask me I can tell you a thing or two 'bout fornication and gluttony. You know what gluttony is?"

"No."

"Gluttony is when some people eat too damn much. Stuff themselves full of food when other people is starving to death and they just go on eating as if it don't matter there ain't enough food for the poor and downtrodden. I was once poor and downtrodden. Hadn't a pot to piss in. Had to fill my belly with anything I could get. You wouldn't believe what starving people ate. Sometimes soup made of tree bark and grass. That's when I swore to God if he let me live I'd go out in the world and preach his Holy word. That's why you see me going from here to there in the service of the Lord. Tell me true. You bin saved?"

"No."

"Bin Baptized?"

"No."

"We'll have to do somethin' about that right away since I'm a Shepherd and you're my Lamb and it's my God-given duty to show you the light. Save your soul for Christ! And that's the truth. That's how come I asked you to ride with me." The Preacher took Berl by the arm. "Now you jus' come with me," he said leading him to the far side of the campsite to the beach of a small lake. Berl resisted, frightened. Struggled to break free. The Preacher walked them into the water. Standing waist deep in the lake he raised his arms and began praying. "Lord I'm asking you to accept this child into Paradise as I wash away his sins."

Berl screamed "No! No! No!" as the Preacher placed one hand in the small of his back bending him over, immersing his head under water.

"I baptize thee in the name of the father, the son and the Holy Ghost" he shouted as Berl broke from his grasp.

Berl ran to his campsite, grabbed his backpack and roller skates and fled into the forest. He had never been in a forest before where threatening shadows concealed unknown dangers as he watched towering trees swaying in the wind sensing the dark mysteries of the wilderness. He remembered stories of children wandering in a forest forever, confused, crying out in despair and feared this could be his fate. Berl turned around and looked for the trail back to the campsite. Only the roar of trucks in the highway told him he was not lost. He would return to the campsite when the Preacher was gone and sit down no longer fearful, lean back against a tree breathing deep, inhaling the pungent odor of a Pine forest wondering: Can this be Paradise?

Paradise was never in a backstage smoke-filled dressing room crowded with admirers hugging and kissing him, applauding and shouting praise for his performance when what he wanted was peace and quiet after the exhaustion of a two hour concert. Watching his parents accept congratulations as if they and not he was the virtuoso seemed unfair.

Dante's Inferno or "The Madhouse" was the unofficial name of New York City's Missing Persons Bureau a bedlam of ringing telephones, chattering printers, and blaring radios where everyone shouted. Some employees proclaimed, after restoring shattered nerves with boilermakers at the local Pub, they had no fear of going to Purgatory for "I've already served my time in Hell!"

Lacking the patience of Job, Sergeant Emiliano Dante sat at his desk staring at a stack of Case Worker Reports. "Enough! Enough of this shit!" he cried out shoving the folders aside, rising from his chair and walking to a coffee pot where he poured a cup of hot black Java. One cup an hour enabled him to survive coping with paper work and hysterical families who demanded what he could not provide. The answer to their prayers. What he did possess, acquired through ten years at the Bureau, was an understanding of boys who ran away from home. "Sometimes they are restless and hungry for adventure," he advised. "And sometimes they are escaping abuse like anger and bullying." He paused to observe the body language of parents often confirming this possibility. "And sometimes," he continued, "they just want to make their grieving families worry thinking you'll be sorry you was so mean to me." After admitting his failure to find their children, pausing for parental disappointment to subside, Sergeant Dante told distraught families "Amnesia is also possible. A boy falls, hits his head and doesn't know who he is or where he's been. And there's also the possibility of foul play, Kidnapping and Murder."

Riva, Berl's mother, glared at Sergeant Dante who leaned back in his chair as she spoke down to him in a well-trained voice. Tall, with the commanding presence of a Wagnerian Diva, she had a voice darkened by pain for she knew the heart-break of an unfulfilled career, of not achieving what she once devoted her life to. Reading her Dossier Sergeant Dante also learned she lived with the sorrow of a dream deferred, disappointment following years striving for perfection. She once dreamed of performing great music and vowed not to allow her son's career to fail as she had failed. Sergeant Dante disliked Jacob, Berl's father, who stopped teaching school to manage his son's career. Booking concerts and interviews, traveling first class on trains and steamships, he relied on Berl to support the family sacrificing a normal childhood for life in Grand Hotels that became Berl's home away from home. Not an admirable parent, Dante thought. Also demanding answers, an intimate friend of the family, Maestro Leonardo was a celebrity Sergeant Dante had seen carving the air with his baton, reaching out like a lover to embrace the orchestra with both arms, singing as he followed the score. Reading his Dossier Sergeant Dante learned mentoring young violinists gave meaning and purpose to Leonardo's life. Blinded by a passion to teach, Maestro Leonardo never sensed the delicacy, the fragility of the boy's personality. He ignored Berl's vulnerability to anger, never saw the face of a child crumple under the onslaught of shouts and abuse, pain and fear. He ignored Berl's attempts to protect himself against such violence with silence, resentment and inevitable rebellion. His parent's emotions crowded Dante's office with anguish. The Sergeant lit another cigarette. Poured himself another cup of coffee while allowing the family to ventilate their fears.

"There's no ransom note," Jacob said. "Not one word. "No phone calls," Riva added, raising a handkerchief to her eyes sobbing.

"I don't believe he has been harmed," Leonardo said. "Who would hurt such a beautiful child?"

"You worked him too hard," Jacob insisted. "Too hard for such a young boy."

"And you booked too many concerts. Promoting him before he was ready," Leonardo replied.

"You both exploited him," Riva shouted. "Money and fame was all you thought about."

"And you?" Leonardo demanded. "Lying about his age. Dressing him like a small boy."

"How else should he look?" Riva asked. "He was a famous child prodigy."

"But not forever," Leonardo said. "Not forever! Boys grow up you know."

The Prodigy

Sergeant Dante interrupted their quarrel. Put down his cigarette and coffee cup. Thoughtful. "Sometimes a man or boy has had enough of the life imposed on him," he explained. "he can't take your shit no more. That's when he says – Give me liberty or give me death and runs away."

Berl's first destination was New York's Greenwich Village, the Mecca of America's Bohemians where Sidewalk Cafes and Bistros serving poets, writers, and musicians provided him with an alternative to an ascetic life performing classical music. Flying the flag of unrestrained sexual and artistic freedom, with "Everything Goes" their Mantra, loud heart-throbbing Jazz proclaimed hope for a better world where free love and compassion replaced fear and hate. Entering a Dance Hall crowded with Shimmy and Charleston dancers, Berl stepped onto the floor and began dancing, his arms opening wide to become part of the bedlam transporting him to another world. His body twisted and turned, swayed back and forth in time to the music's relentless beat, his heart pounding he had his first intoxicating taste of freedom listening to the voices of Troubadours. Lonely voices expressing the emotions of their time. Voices crying out in pain. Voices protesting. Voices asking, "Brother can you spare a dime?" In a small Café theater Berl heard a singer say what was in his heart forever changing his life.

"I want to live, and know the joys of existence
It all depends on me
I want to live Yes!
I want to live,
Before I die."

TWO

Sergeant Dante could not believe his eyes. He'd seen prison cells furnished better and more inviting than Berl's bedroom. Riva objected to anyone searching Berl's room for clues to what Berl was feeling or thinking before he disappeared. She stood in the doorway and protested: "You're invading our privacy," she said in her operatic voice. "You have no right to do this."

Sergeant Dante opened a briefcase and pulled out a large envelope. "Here's a Court Order. A Warrant," he said quietly. Riva turned and stepped out of the doorway refusing to be served as Sergeant Dante followed her into the house. "Please show me his room," he insisted. Riva surrendered, leading him up a narrow flight of stairs to a room in the attic. She unlocked the door. "Is this room always locked?" Sergeant Dante asked.

"Only when needed," Riva replied. "to maintain discipline."

No posters or photographs decorated the walls. A sleeping pad on an iron cot with a thin woolen blanket was next to an old maple bureau, a music stand, a record player and a floor lamp with only one bulb working when he reached out and turned it on. On a desk sheet music and stacks of records were arranged in some kind of order. A Hermit's Cell, Dante thought. Solitary confinement. Certainly not a room for a boy his age. He looked up at the attic's narrow window wondering had it ever been cleaned?

He sat on the cot and tried to imagine what it would be like to live in this barren room. Friendless. Alone with his thoughts practicing his violin. A prisoner of his mother's ambitions. He asked to see the driveway where Berl fell and broke his arm. Located between two adjacent homes, a paved alley went from the garage to the street. A hundred yards of concrete. Walking down the alley, Sergeant Dante carefully examined the pavement.

"Where did Berl fall and break his arm?" he asked.

"Over here," Jacob replied. "You can still see where I washed away the blood. There was a lot of blood."

Sergeant Dante knelt and placed his hand on the road. "Was it always this clean?" he asked.

"Not always," Jacob replied. "After Berl fell I've been sweeping."

Sergeant Dante smiled. "Was Berl a good skater?" he asked.

"He was learning" Jacob said. "Had trouble with balance. He was not very athletic."

Sergeant Dante looked down at the road. "It wouldn't take much of an obstruction to make him fall," he said quietly. "A small stone. Some gravel. You can't roller skate on gravel." Dante reached down and picked up several small stones scattering them on the road. Jacob turned and stared at Dante.

"What are you doing? What are you saying?" He demanded.

Dante paused a moment wondering about Jacob's reaction. "I'm saying it is possible there was no accident."

Jacob raised his hand to his face, shaking his head. "Oy Vey! Oy Vey! My poor boy! Who would do such a thing?" he cried out.

"A good question," Sergeant Dante replied. "A good question."

The majestic Mississippi, the "Old Man River" of song and story, flows from the Canadian border to the Gulf of Mexico dividing the settled east from the western territories that became the United States of America. Emigrants in covered wagons fulfilled our nation's "Manifest Destiny", their heroic trek ending at the Pacific where they left behind their past to build a new nation. St. Louis, "The Gateway to the West" welcomed and tolerated all kinds of travelers. Ear shattering music blasting from a high-decibel "Boom Box" announced the arrival of a road-battered Hearse spray painted with psychedelic colors driving across the river into the setting sun. Squinting into the glare, eyes half-closed, the driver sang the lyrics of a popular song pounding the steering wheel with his hand to follow the wild pulsating beat. "Yeah! Yeah! Yeah!" he shouted. "Yeah! Yeah! Yeah! Dark curtains covered the side and back windows of the Hearse. Two air mattresses, a Coleman camping stove. A cooler and a record player furnished the interior, the home of the driver and his passenger. On the wall separating the driver's compartment from the living area, next to a display of publicity photographs, a Billboard poster proclaimed in very large letters: "RUDI-THE RED HOT FIDDLER."

Switching off the music the driver turned and reached back to open the small glass window behind his seat. "Wake Up! Wake Up! You sleepy head," he sang and laughed sounding the car's horn again and again. "It's time! It's time to get out of bed! Live! Love! Laugh and be happy!" he shouted hoping for a response from his sleeping passenger. "It's your turn to drive," the driver explained. "The sun is blinding me." Berl rose from his sleeping bag, sat up and rubbed sleep out of his eyes. He put on a sweatshirt and baseball cap as the Hearse pulled over to the side of the road where he replaced the driver behind the wheel. When asked at a Truck Stop food counter if he could drive he lied. He had never driven before. Rudi the driver, leaned back in his seat, closed his eyes and said: "Keep it under sixty. This old bitch ain't what she used to be." Berl nodded confidently, concentrating on steering, his foot gently pressing the accelerator. Not much to driving, he thought. Not much at all. He had showered at the Truck Stop, finished a good meal when the driver wearing coveralls and cowboy hat approached and offered him a ride. The aches and pains in his legs demanded rest, and riding for a few days with someone to talk to would be welcome. In the next hundred miles he heard about Rudi's career as a "Barker" or "Pitchman" travelling to State Fairs where he competed and won Hot Fiddlin' contests and played the violin at Line and Square dances. The driver enjoyed telling Berl of standing on a box at the entrance to THE SNAKE WOMAN's tent shouting: "She walks!... She talks!... She wiggles!... She crawls on her belly like a Reptile! Hurry! Hurry! The next show in ten minutes! And only ten cents!... One tenth part of a dollar!" A born story-teller, Rudi had the full belly laugh of a Comedian.

An Entertainer. A source of popular wisdom. "There's a sucker born every minute," he said. "Old PT Barnum was right! Damn right! And if you want a really good laugh go see the Pig Calling contest! He raised his hands to his mouth forming a megaphone and called... SOEE SOEE SOEE! HERE PIG! PIG! PIG! ... inhaling to catch his breath he paused and laughed saying "It's funnier than Yodeling or husband calling." Imitating the powerful voice of a woman competing in the event he hollered in a high-pitched Farm wife's voice... "ELMER!... ELMER!... ELMER!" his voice rising, becoming shrill. "ELMER!" he shouted again and again... T-E-L-E-P-H-O-N-E!"

Sergeant Emiliano Dante, also known as "The Brain", despised listening to distraught families asking questions. He often heard their pleading voices in his sleep. "We're doing everything humanly possible" he always replied. "Following every clue. Pursuing every fact." An exhausting dialogue. He was happy just sitting at his desk, eyes closed, following his intuitions. He pushed back his chair, ignored the telephone's flashing lights and paced around his office. In the evening, after the day shift left the Bureau, Dante locked his office door, spread a small rug on the floor and bent over to stand on his head. With his arms out-stretched to maintain balance, his legs raised towards the ceiling, blood saturating his brain, Dante did his best thinking. In this inverted position he solved the Bureau's most intractable cases believing no Dossier should ever be interred in the Missing Persons Morgue. Sooner or later clues emerged sparking his insatiable devotion to facts. Nothing but the facts. A recognizable signature on a hotel registration card located Judge Casey alive and well living in Topeka Kansas under a false name. An Embezzler's habit of writing bad checks, a Bigamist's joy in maintaining multiple families, and a Forger's pride in his handwriting enabled Dante to solve their disappearances confirming his belief missing persons were never missing only misplaced. Standing on his head, with his mind nourished, speculating about Berl's disappearance, Dante recalled a leading Figure Skater knee-capped by a Competitor. Yes. No doubt. Ambition can be the root of all Evil and Berl's broken arm improved other violinists chances of winning prestigious International Music competitions.

During the American mid-west's long hard winters, only a single strand of barbed wire at the Canadian border shielded these states from the Arctic air flowing south to prolong suffering. Housebound for weeks, families opened storm windows and doors, closeted wool Parkas and rubber snow boots anticipating the arrival of the annual Spring floods. The blazing hot summers were endured sustained by expectations of the coming harvest months celebrated at State Fairs exhibiting prize-winning livestock, astounding displays of produce, and such entertainments as Ferris Wheels, Merry-Go-Rounds, Harness racing and enticing Tents where sword and fire swallowers competed for attention with such exotic "Girlie Shows" as Rosita dancing across the stage with a flock of Doves, fluttering white wings enveloped in the folds of her flowing dress. A Steam Calliope's joyous music quickened all hearts, raised all spirits as farm boys and girl touring the Fairgrounds consumed boxes of buttered popcorn. In all his travelling Berl had never seen anything so exciting. Visiting the exhibits and attractions he failed to win a Kewpie doll at the target shooting range, lost money in a Con Man's Shell game, but succeeded in calling out the weight of the Fat Lady sitting in a chair suspended from a scale smiling at his lucky guess. He was shocked and saddened by the popular "Coon Ball" game enjoyed by a sadistic audience attracted by a Barker crying "Three balls for a quarter!" With puffed out cheeks he shouted: "Three balls for only twenty-five cents!" Berl turned and saw a large canvas target thirty feet from a countertop covered with baseballs. In the center of the Bulls-eye a young black face grinned, eyes rolling in mock terror. "Hit the Coon! Win an expensive prize!" the Barker shrilled holding up a stuffed Panda Bear. "Be a real Man!" he cried out again. "Show your Old Lady your powerful pitching arm!" At the target the black boy grinned. The crowd hooted and hollered anticipating a bloody outcome. "Three balls for twenty-five cents! Three balls for only a quarter!" the Barker shouted as a tall pock-marked youth stepped to the counter, fisted a baseball and carefully aimed at the Bulls-eye winding up for a powerful pitch. The boy at the target closed his eyes. The crowd hushed into gleeful silence as Berl turned away unable to witness the horror.

Maestro Leonardo, identified by critics as the "Pied Piper" of the music world celebrated the joy of making music on radio programs inspiring children fascinated by his persuasive personality.

The Prodigy

Waving his arms, his long hair trailing behind him as he lectured, his appeal to the young to aspire to a life dedicated to creating beauty could not be denied. Indeed music school enrollments soared, hopeful parents dreaming of musical careers for their children gladly paid exorbitant tuitions. That so many children lacked talent or motivation was ignored. Sergeant Dante's list of suspects included the Maestro although in his judgment Leonardo seemed a remote possibility. Berl's success demonstrated Leonardo's genius for recognizing and developing talent. He had an instinctive feeling for artistic temperament. To damage his reputation as a successful mentor was unthinkable. Yet Berl did abandon the career Leonardo had worked so hard to inspire. Leonardo's passionate interviews praising Berl revealed his love for his pupil. Like the Greek Sculpture enamored by the statue he created, Maestro Leonardo was often in tears when expressing his love for Berl. Certainly the flame of his teachings and thought could never be extinguished in his most promising student.

Studying Berl's publicity photographs Sergeant Dante was struck by his resemblance to a Botticelli Angel. Eyes uplifted to heaven. An innocent smile. Hair flowing down to shoulders. Sergeant Dante put down the photographs to allow his feelings to subside. No doubt about it. Berl was indeed beautiful and seductive. Happily married with several children, Leonardo was a controversial artist who suffered blacklisting for his political beliefs, prurient gossip about his personal behavior, and negative reviews from antagonistic critics. Often wearing a cape instead of an overcoat, the Maestro projected the Romantic appearance of a character from a previous century. A Man of Mystery. What was his relationship with Berl really like Sergeant Dante wondered? Children do run away to escape abuse.

Located at the end of the Midway, the only free attraction at the State Fair was THE CHILDREN'S STORY TENT with vividly painted canvas walls illustrating such childhood tales as *Cinderella, little Red Riding Hood* and *Jack and The Beanstalk.* Strolling past Barkers pitching luring attractions, Berl stopped to watch *Bozo* the clown at the entrance to the children's tent singing and dancing and waving his arms to attract an audience. A Player Piano inside the tent accompanied performers using Hand Puppets to act out stories that evoked wonder and surprise in the audience. At each frightening moment in a story the children became silent and fearful covering their eyes with their hands. Then, after minutes of prolonged suspense, goodness and justice prevailed as the children screamed with delight at a world where every ending is a happy one. Entering the tent, watching the Puppets, Berl was surprised. He had never seen anything so thrilling. Denied children's books, these stories were unknown to him as his parents considered Fairy Tales too frightening for a sensitive child. Attracted to the Puppet show by a power beyond his control, he returned day after day until he lost all track of time and place. The pure soul-stirring voice of Cinderella singing *Someday My Prince Will Come* awakened feelings he never knew he contained. Feelings of tenderness, beauty and passion. Here in this tent he found the sweet mystery of life. A discovery so overwhelming he became mute. Speechless. A boy in love.

One night, with the steam Calliope silent and the Fairgrounds abandoned after a long day of fun and games, Berl entered the darkened children's tent as if drawn to his destiny. From the stage at the rear of the tent, Cinderella smiled at him. He imagined she was calling out to him as he slowly walked towards her mesmerized. Berl stopped for a moment, staring at her, trembling, awed by the beauty of her flowing dress, her hair crowned with a sparkling Tiara. Thrilled by her radiance he began crying tears of joy. Then, as if in a wondrous dream he heard the pure and affectionate voice of the Puppet ask "Are you the boy travelling with Rudi the Fiddler?"

"Yes." Berl replied, happy Cinderella spoke to him.

"Come to see the Prince rescue me?" she asked.

"Yes! Yes!" he insisted. "I like how your story ends."

"There's a movie about me, you know," Cinderella said. "A love story. Everybody loves love stories even though they are sad and filled with grief and woe."

"Why is that?" Berl asked. "You seem so happy."

"Believe me I have loved and I know. But not my story. My Prince always comes to save me and we live happily ever after like in a Fairy Tale." Cinderella paused a moment. Stared at him. "Have you ever been in love?" she asked. "Had your heart beat faster? Been possessed thinking about the love of your life? Been awake all night wondering does she or does she not love you?"

"Never," Berl replied. "Never."

"If you've never been in love you're only half alive. Why I fall in love twenty performances a day. The only way to live."

Berl thought about this possibility a moment. Hesitating. "How do you fall in love?" he asked.

"It's not easy," Cinderella said. "You'll have your heart broken. Burn with jealousy. Be overcome by anger and rage. Commit crimes of passion. Murder! Falling head over heels in love can be a terrible experience."

"I'm not afraid," Berl said.

"You jump into a bottom-less abyss," Cinderella replied. Her voice darkening as she remembered a lost love. "It's a long way down before you hit rock bottom. But first you have to have somebody to love. Somebody to give your heart and soul to."

"Like you?" Berl pleaded. "Can I fall in love with you?"

"Me? I wouldn't if I were you. You don't know what can happen," Cinderella insisted. "All you now see is what's in front of a beautiful velvet curtain. A dancing and singing Puppet. The Devil's candy!"

"Yes! Yes!" Berl pleaded. "You can be the love of my life!"

"Foolish boy! What do you think you'll find behind the curtain?" Cinderella asked. Shaking her head. Suddenly sad. "Nothing but grief and strife. A lover's life."

Judge Horatio Silver, a vehement defender of civil liberties, initially refused Sergeant Dante's request for a Court Order to investigate Jacob's finances. He believed invading a citizen's privacy required circumstances Dante failed to demonstrate. Staring down from the bench over the top of his eyeglasses, the Judge ruled in an unusually loud voice: "Invading the privacy of a customer's Stock Trading account is no different from kicking in his front door. It is a surreptitious entry and this Court considers such actions illegal."

Dante controlled his disappointment. This was not his first request for additional investigative power. In a quiet voice he pleaded: "Your Honor I believe a boy's life is in jeopardy. He is a missing person we have been unable to locate. A possible Kidnapping."

"Have you received a ransom note?" Judge Silver asked. "A phone call demanding money?"

"No, Your Honor."

"Then why do you suggest Kidnapping?" The Judge asked. "Why not murder?"

"Murder is also possible," Dante replied. "A consequence of our failure to locate a boy who we estimate has earned almost a half a million dollars in the past four years."

"An estimate is not a fact," Judge Silver replied. "This court deals only in facts."

"Your Honor we have been unable to obtain a proper accounting of the boy's financial affairs managed by his father."

"What are you suggesting?" asked the Judge.

"Possible embezzlement. Concealed extraordinary losses," Dante said. "The father is known to be a compulsive gambler."

"With his son's money?" Judge Silver asked. Frowning.

"Yes, Your Honor," Dante explained. "And It is possible a disappointed and grieving boy ran away

24

to keep from making more money for his father to lose."

"Yes, it is possible," Judge Silver said as he reluctantly signed the Court Order.

Rudi was indeed the hottest of the Red Hot Fiddlers. His fast playing *Turkey In The Straw* wore out Jig dancers struggling to keep up with his furious pace. Heads high, backs straight, moving only their legs, shoes pounding the wooden dance floor, they danced faster and faster to meet the challenge of Rudi's Fiddling. The crowd clapped their hands and stamped their feet encouraging more high stepping speed from the Fiddler and the line of Jig dancers. Exhausted dancers soon withdrew from the competition until only one survived. Rudi put down his Fiddle and walked across the dance floor to embrace the winner as he collapsed into his arms. Rudi held up the dancer's hand proclaiming a hard-won victory. The crowd cheered.

For several weeks Berl postponed resuming his westward journey. The State Fair's, entertainments, the fun and games, were seductive. Hard to resist. Impossible to leave now he was in love living in a blissful state with someone to talk to. Someone to listen to him. Someone to share confidences with. He could not give up talking to Cinderella. His first love, the love of his life. Abandoning her would break his heart. No doubt he would love Cinderella forever. One night, unable to find words to express his love, he borrowed Rudi's violin to serenade Cinderella with the language he knew best. The language of the human heart. Music. Entering the children's tent, standing in front of the stage Berl began playing *None But The Lonely Heart Can Know My Anguish* with a slow mournful tempo he poured his soul into. Surely, without speaking, she would recognize his great undeniable love for her. He continued playing, every note accompanying a beat of his heart. He was enthralled.

Then, from behind the curtain, responding to his playing, he heard uncontrollable heart-breaking sobs, a cry of pain and sorrow and suffering. Alarmed. He stopped playing. "What have I done?" he asked. The sobbing continued. "I won't play anymore," he promised. "I didn't know you didn't like music," he explained.

"I love music," the voice behind the curtain said. "I love your playing."

"Then what did I do wrong?" Berl asked, trembling. Fearful.

"Nothing, the sobbing voice behind the curtain said. "You did nothing wrong. Your song reminded me of my anguish. My lonely heart."

"How can that be?" Berl asked. "How can you be lonely with so many children coming to see you every day? They love you," he insisted. "They all love you."

"They love Cinderella." The voice behind the curtain said. "Not me."

"I don't understand" Berl said, confused.

"Nobody has ever loved me," the voice behind the curtain said. "Nobody will ever love me. I'm just unlucky in love."

"You're young and beautiful and that's why the Prince falls in love with you. And I love you!" Berl insisted passionately. "I will love you forever."

"You're a foolish boy," the voice said. "You must not give your heart away to everyone you love."

"I've never loved anyone before. You are my first love. The love of my life."

"Then only God can rescue you from your foolishness," the voice said. "You have no idea who you are in love with. A beautiful voice? A singing and dancing Puppet? A dream? A Fairy Tale of love and happiness? When you fall in love your troubles begin."

Berl began crying. Tears filled his eyes. "No he shouted. No! What you say can't be true!" Desperate. Shaking his head he reached out impulsively and grabbed the curtain in his fist.

"Don't do that," the voice behind the curtain pleaded. "Don't open the curtain. You'll be sorry if you do!" Berl hesitated. Waited a moment, unable to make up his mind. Then, reaching out he tore open the curtain and found the Circus's famous Fat Lady, handkerchief in hand, drying her eternal tears of sorrow.

THREE

Legally defined "Persons of Interest" are not always interesting, Sergeant Emiliano Dante thought after listening to Riva's telephone taps. Berl's mother, a non-stop talker, filled hours of tapes with the self-centered chatter of a vain thoughtless woman. Her telephone was wielded like a Maestro's baton lecturing friends who listened patiently and rarely got a chance to respond. She's an ego trip, Sergeant Dante concluded as he continued searching for possible clues of her involvement in Berl's disappearance. An exercise in futility. Jacob, Berl's father, was definitely worth recording. Calls to Stock Brokers, Gambling Casino Managers, accountants, Lawyers and Escort services revealed a dissolute, irresponsible, out of control life style suggesting Jacob was capable of almost any desperate act. Casino Croupiers called Jacob a hard drinking "heavy hitter, and heavy loser". An easy "Mark" welcomed wherever he laid down his thousand dollar chips. Sergeant Dante decided, as he signed the order requesting more surveillance, what we now know about Jacob is incomplete. Something vital was missing. So watch and wait was the order of the day.

For Agents working in "Dante's Inferno", New York's Missing Persons Bureau, candid photographs and telephone tapes of Maestro Leonardo's Gay flamboyant life were entertaining revealing unrestrained participation in an underworld of drugs and sex. Lording over his friends, surrounded by adoring sycophants, Maestro Leonardo granted or withheld his favors kissing and embracing his favorite of the moment. Some were potential lovers, or political activists, or violent demonstrators with numerous arrests. Sergeant Dante recognized several well-known criminals, now considered celebrities, active leaders of gangs and syndicates that corrupted the city he loved. Maestro Leonardo was certainly a "Person of Interest."

Surveillance of Menahim, winner of the prestigious Queen Elizabeth International Violin competition when Berl was unable to perform, revealed nothing questionable. Dante was impressed by Menahim's disciplined hardworking daily struggle to master his instrument. Certainly as a "Person of Interest" he was, and should be, of no interest at all.

More than two thousand mourners attended Ziggy Goldfarb's funeral. As a famous Impresario he presented musicians, opera stars, symphony Orchestras and Ballets to adoring world-wide audiences. Known for his ability to discover and promote outstanding talent, "Goldfarb Entertainment" was incomparable. A short, portly figure, wearing an enormous halo of white hair, Ziggy looked like an enthusiastic child delighted by the world of culture and intelligence that surrounded him wherever he travelled. A surrogate grandfather hugging and kissing Berl whenever they met, he provided the affection withheld by his austere parents winning Berl's adoration as the one most responsible for his success. Dismayed when learning of Riva's attempt to break their contract with Goldfarb, Berl was conflicted. Life without Goldfarb's love was unthinkable. And when coached by a Lawyer to testify in support of his mother's Lawsuit he was silent. Unable to speak.

"Were you always satisfied with the Hotel and travel arrangements Goldfarb provided?" the Lawyer asked, leaning over Berl. His smooth voice friendly. Paternal. Berl pretended not to understand the question. "You know very well, "Riva interrupted rudely. "Goldfarb did not always give us the very best accommodations." Berl slowly shook his head. Pressed his lips together. Remained silent. The Lawyer again leaned over Berl holding his hand like a forgiving father. "I'm sure you had no way of knowing Goldfarb was taking financial advantage of you and your mother."

Again Berl said nothing. Turned away. Staring down at his tightly clasped hands.

The Lawyer continued. Insistent. "You must understand demanding a better contract with Goldfarb, increasing your share of your earnings, is smart and right."

Again Riva interrupted. "We are only thinking of what is best for you," she cried out sobbing. Berl continued his silence. Then he turned to look at his mother and saw a stranger, someone he had never seen before.

Everybody loves a Parade, particularly on Memorial Day, July Fourth, and Veterans' Day when our country's founding idea "E Pluribus Unum - Making one nation out of many" is celebrated. On the State Fair's last day, enthusiastic crowds applauded the splendiferous uniforms of the

Marching Band and dancing "Pom Pom" girls escorting the Grand Marshall, Governor "Bull" Hominy graciously bowing and waving at spectators as he led the line of marchers. Waves of laughter greeted *Bozo* the Clown leading an Elephant and a Camel down the Midway followed by two Midgets sweeping up animal flop as the crowd shouted approval of their fastidiousness. Strongman Samson, bending an iron bar with his hands led teams of tumbling Acrobats, Freaks, and Contortionists along the Parade route accompanied by a high-pitched Steam Calliope celebrating a day when having fun was Life's only activity.

To insure re-election in the next Primary, Governor "Bull" Hominy brightened the closing ceremonies with one of his dramatic "Stump" speeches said to be more entertaining than a barrel of monkeys fighting over a banana. Obsessed, some thought demented, the Governor waved his arms and pounded the palm of his hand with his fist, his florid face bleeding sweat as he pledged: "Re-elect me and I will continue to fight for the poor man – all poor men – black and white – men who gotta have a chance to have a home -- a job – a decent education for their children in a country where every man is a King but no one wears a crown!" Raising a red bandanna to his face, drying his wet forehead, pausing for the applause to subside the "Bull" roared again and again: "There will be a Chicken in every Pot when we share our Country's fabulous wealth! Yes Siree I tell you there will be a Chicken in every pot and prosperity will be just around the corner!" Shouting agreement with his promise, the hysterical audience, now a chorus of Fools screamed: "Thank God for 'Bull' Hominy! Thank God for 'Bull' Hominy! Thank God For 'Bull' Hominy!"

Berl knew nothing about "Bull" Hominy, elections, Politics, or Politicians. He was glad to escape from the Fair's excitement and political tumult happy to be Roller Skating through farmlands where the corn does indeed grow as high as an Elephant's eye and every morning is beautiful. Seeing the sun rise and set every day with fair weather Cumulus clouds floating overhead he experienced the intoxicating freedom of an adventurer pursuing an unknown destiny. Quo Vadis? Where are you going? were questions of no concern. The sun and wind caressing his face, watching Hawks soaring high overhead on out-stretched wings filled his soul with ecstasy. He felt weightless, floating on air, free of all worry and care. Yes! There were many poor people without hope, homes or jobs unable to educate their children. Sad but true. But what could he do for them? And what about the Governor promising every man a King? And no one with a Crown? And a Chicken in every Pot? How is that possible? Yes indeed it's good to get away from such men and their speeches. And Yes! Yes! he felt fine just roller skating along a highway leading him to his tomorrow.

Tomorrow? Hadn't thought much about tomorrow, Berl said to himself. Yes! Tomorrow is a good idea, something to think about. Yesterday was the problem. If only I could forget my past. A stone burdening my heart. As Berl skated down the highway he had conversations with his parents. Now he was not their prisoner he could think his own thoughts, live his own life. Say what he truly felt. Let me live! Please let me live! You have had your lives. Let me have mine. Yes. My Tomorrow is a good idea. But a tomorrow without music? Without perfecting the gift inside me? Without achieving possibilities I didn't know I possessed?

Yes, concealed behind every curtain is a Fat Lady with a beautiful voice breaking my heart. And a Preacher leading people astray. And a Fiddler entertaining them while a Demagogue makes promises he could never keep. Will they be my tomorrow?

The odds for other Competitors to win the Gold Medal at Belgium's Queen Elizabeth's International Music Competition were dramatically raised by Berl's disappearance. Standing on his head, Sergeant Dante focused his enriched mind on identifying the contestant who would get the most advantage from Berl's absence. A violinist desperate to win the world's most prestigious musical award who would prefer Berl be unable to compete. Perhaps fearing for his safety, Berl ran away from this threat?

Fleeing the Shtetls of Eastern Europe where many rooftops had Fiddlers, mastering the violin was a passport to freedom, an escape from the poverty of "The Pale of Settlement" where Russian Jews were permitted to live. They walked or rode in horse drawn carts journeying to the enlightened Western world where minds were free of the rigors of traditional religious dogma. Parents dreaming of wealth and celebrity for their children devoted a large portion of their meager income to violin lessons beginning at the age of four or five. And to the cities of western Europe and America arrived hundreds, perhaps thousands of hopeful Prodigies their childhoods disciplined by long hours of study and practice.

Sergeant Dante's Italian blood thrilled to the astonishing voices of Enrico Caruso, Galla Curci, and Franco Corelli. He preferred the Grand opera glories of Pagliacci to the soft lyrical beauty of the concert violin. He was surprised at the number of aspiring young performers competing for the attention needed to win violin scholarships. And they arrived not only from Western Europe but from China, Japan and Korea. An International talent invasion with the energy and discipline that would make their dreams become real.

Yes, Sergeant Dante concluded, an ambitious competitor, driven mad by exhausting years of study and practice, desperate for success, could do the unthinkable.

Berl rolled over in his sleeping bag hoping for another hour recovering from yesterday's skating. "God damn it! "he groaned as a loud rendition of *God Bless America* echoing around the campsite made more sleep impossible. Rubbing his eyes he slid out of the bag, sat up and looked around to see parked nearby a large Greyhound Bus with VOTE FOR "BULL" HOMINY and an American flag painted on one side. A Bullhorn on the roof attacked the peace and quiet of a summer morning. Taking a sweatshirt and shorts from his backpack he dressed quickly. After breakfasting on Granola bars and an orange Berl strapped on his skates eager to flee the unwelcome intrusion of a political campaigner. Rudi the Red Hot Fiddler stepped out of the Bus, raised his arm and waved at Berl.

"I thought that was you," he shouted. "Been looking all over for you. Just don't understand why you left the Fairgrounds without so much as a good by. That wasn't friendly!"

"I had to get going," Berl replied. "I have a long way to go."

"What's your rush?" Rudi shouted. "You got the rest of your life to get to California. Why I know some folks get to California and don't like it. Couldn't breathe the air. Did you know that? They got smog in California. Yes siree Bob you can take my word for it. You got better things to do with your life than go to California and choke to death on smog. Now if you'll take off them damn roller skates and listen to me I got a proposition for you. Believe you me a real hot ticket to your future."

"What's a proposition?" Berl asked.

"An opportunity that comes once in a lifetime and if you miss it, it will never come again. Now I always know a good proposition when I see one and when Governor Hominy asked me to join his campaign for the Senate of the United States of America I didn't think twice about it. I said yes! And now I'm warming up the crowds with my Fiddle wherever he stops to speak. Red Hot Fiddlin gets lots of votes!"

"Why is that?" Berl asked. His curiosity aroused.

"Well when you get people excited they just don't think about what you're saying. That's what politics is all about. Getting people so excited they don't know which end is up. Which is why I have a proposition for you. Nothing draws a crowd better than a Red Hot Fiddlin competition between two Fiddlers sawing away on their Fiddles like they had a stick of dynamite up their ass. And you could be the other Fiddler."

"I don't know anything about fiddling." Berl replied.

"Ain't much to it," Rudi said and turned to walk back to the Bus. Returning with a violin and a bow he held the Fiddle to his chest and moved the bow over a string. "Why you just press your finger down on this here string and saw back and forth with the bow until your arm is about to fall off and when you really get going, stamping your foot and thinking you can't play no faster you just press down on this here other string and it's like you get a second wind running a race. There's no tellin how fast you can go when you get red hot."

"Rudi!" A young girl in blue jeans a sweatshirt and dark glasses shouted from the Bus's doorway. "Who are you talking to?"

"An old friend." Rudi replied. "The one I been looking for. The boy roller skating to California."

"Is he mad?" she asked, stepping out of the Bus. Questioning him. "Out of his mind?"

"Just young and misguided," Rudi said. "I'm trying to set him strait. Keep him from wasting his life."

"I'm glad to hear that," she said relieved. Shaking her head. "He could get killed on the highway. Why don't you ask him to ride with us?"

"That's what I'm doin' only I think maybe he's stubborn."

"Sorry to hear that," she said, returning to the Bus. "Some kids learn everything the hard way."

"You can say that again," Rudi replied.

"Who's that?" Berl asked excited by the strange beauty and voice of the girl. "That's Cora, the Governor's daughter," Rudi explained. "The crowd loves when she tells about going blind and her mother dying and her Daddy raising her all by his self. I tell you there's a lot of sobbin' and cryin' when she speaks."

"Well," Berl said considering Rudi's proposition a moment turning to look at the Bus. "Maybe teaching me to Fiddle would be a lot of fun."

Later that day, Berl enjoyed sitting beside Cora as the Bus travelled to the next campaign stop. He had never been this close to the physical presence of a girl before. Seeing her staring out the window he asked: "Why are you always looking out the window"

"Watching the scenery," she replied with a sweet gentle smile. "But you are blind," Berl said, staring at her dark sun glasses. "I can see," she insisted. Nodding her head.

"How's that possible," Berl asked incredulous.

"Close your eyes." she said. "Close your eyes and you'll find out."

"What do you mean?" Berl replied. "What are you saying?"

"Close your eyes and tell me what you see," she demanded.

"Nothing," Berl insisted "I don't see anything."
"You know what a tree looks like even though your eyes are closed?" she asked. "Or a forest? Or a lake? Or a sunset or a sunrise?"
"Certainly," Berl replied. "That's because you remember what they look like and I remember everything I saw before I went blind. I see with my mind's eye. My memory. My imagination. I see more than some people who are not blind. And when the Doctor told me I would never see again I told him he was wrong! Absolutely wrong! For as long as I live I will never stop seeing! Never! For one does not see with the eyes, one sees with the mind. I feel the wind on my face and know it will be rain or sunshine. I hear your voice and see your face. I only have to reach out and touch something to know what it looks like."
"So you really can see?" Berl said. Shaking his head. Still not believing her.
"Yes," she replied. "And lots of people who can see are really blind."

"How dare Sergeant Dante suggest with his impertinent questions I am not a good mother? What can a man possibly know about being a mother? That despicable little man with his little authority who I must endure until Berl is found. Oh my child! My child! My most precious possession. A gift of God I carried and fed for nine months of happy expectation. What would my little baby be like I wondered feeling him moving and kicking inside me like he could hardly wait to be born. There's nothing more wonderful than motherhood! And it's no surprise he's run away. He was restless even before he came out of me. Not for one second, one minute, one hour was I unaware of his existence before he was born. Always moving, moving, crawling across floors, struggling to stand, staggering forward to God knows where tottering on his shaky legs, crying out the first time he walked across the room. And when I sang to him he opened his eyes looking at me surprised, laughing, smiling, and making baby sounds, the only language he could speak. And he ate me alive biting my nipples. Sucking me dry. Caressing my breasts like a young lover. What joy! How I hungered for more! A passion greater than reaching a high note in the greatest aria ever written! A love song! A duet! And I thought he would be mine forever. But that is not possible. A child learns there is more in this world than a mother who teaches him words, and when he speaks everything has a name. A place. An existence beyond his family. I held him close to me as long as possible. I cried the first time I cut his hair. I enameled his first pair of shoes. I hoarded photographs for the distant day when he would no longer be the boy I wanted to remember forever. He had a voice and a mind and a talent, a great gift and a treasure I cultivated, nourished and disciplined with my love, my passion, my devotion. And now that horrid Sergeant Dante shows no respect, no understanding of who and what I am. What I am going through. What I must endure until he finds my son. Oh what a terrible thing it is to lose a child!"

Governor "Bull" Hominy's Campaign Bus brought exciting political entertainment to every County in the State with a powerful Bull Horn blaring several verses of a musical Trio's rendition of his raucous theme song "God Bless 'Bull' Hominy! God Bless 'Bull' Hominy." Cheering crowds gathered on athletic fields and village Greens as the Bus arrived like a ship voyaging a sea of American flags. An Honor Guard of American Legionnaires saluted the Governor's appearance with drums and bugles and military honors. Boy Scouts waved signs welcoming the State's favorite son while screaming hysterical teen-age girls became uncontrollable as Governor Hominy emerged from the door of the Bus to acknowledge their greeting.

This is America, this is really America Berl thought looking out the Bus window excited by campaign stops. Travelling around the State with Cora beside him holding hands, he enjoyed their friendship as she explained her father's strategy of going face to face with voters, shaking hands, kissing babies and becoming someone familiar to crowds of admirers. "This is democracy," Cora explained. "Grass Roots democracy. This is how you get elected to run the best State in the best Country on Earth." Thrilled by their shared intimacy Berl pressed his body closer to Cora wishing campaigning would never end. And every evening, after consuming enormous quantities of Beer and Barbecue a crowd gathered around Rudi who Fiddled and called instructions for Square Dancers driven by endless alcoholic energy.

Standing on a Table, Governor "Bull" Hominy gave the crowd what they had been waiting for. Shouting in a high-pitched voice, waving his arms, pounding his fist into the palm of his hand he cried out: "Every man a King" with the audience responding "And no man wears a Crown." Lowering his voice to subdue the crowd's raucous mood, he promised to "keep poor hardworking Americans from fighting rich men's wars." The crowd cheered and applauded interrupting his speech, stamping their feet until he raised his hand pleading to continue. "When I'm elected I'll make sure this country is governed by real red-blooded Americans for and by Americans. Let the British and the French and the Bolsheviks fight their ungodly wars. Until the day I die I'll lead the only fight worth fighting. The War on Poverty. The crowd exploded shouting: "Fight Poverty! Fight Poverty! Fight Poverty!"

Pouring himself another glass of water the Governor carefully wiped his lips with a red bandana. Then, speaking slowly, deliberately, his sweat-stained face reddening, with a renewed burst of energy he pounded his fist into the palm of his hand shouting: "We must and we will take our country back from the English Bankers and the Jews. They are our misfortune! Our misfortune."

A motorcycle escort of "Bull's Rough Riders" with sirens blaring, preceded his Campaign Bus speeding across the State. In uniforms of white shirts, dark sunglasses, brightly polished boots, with pistols holstered on their belts, they entertained astonished crowds with demonstrations of skillful motorcycle maneuvers. Moving slowly towards the spectators, a squadron of fifty riders divided into two divisions separating to form a large circle. Then, with increasing speed, their headlights flashing, their exhausts roaring, they became two lines of cyclists alternately and precisely crossing in front of each other as the crowd applauded and cheered. Then the two divisions re-formed into a single column riding past the Governor who waved and cheered and saluted their skill. Then the moving parade of motorcycles stopped. The roaring engines silenced. Assembling in front of Governor Hominy, standing at attention beside their motorcycles, the "Rough Riders" raised their arms and swore undying allegiance to their Commander.

Berl had never seen anything so spectacular. He cheered and applauded and stamped his feet responding to the uncontrolled frenzy of the spectators. It was as if his entire body, heart, soul and mind had become one with a wild mob. Then suddenly calm, he turned to Cora and asked: "Does this happen at every campaign stop?" Cora laughed. "Whenever the Riders come and do their show. They'll make my father President someday. People love a Circus. Give them bread and a Circus and they'll vote for you forever." Berl turned and stared at Cora trying to understand her thought. "Is this a good thing?" he asked. "Certainly!" Cora replied. "Is there any other way of getting elected?" Cora continued, lecturing Berl as if to a child. "My Father gives people hope when they are in despair. When they are ashamed of their ignorance and poverty he restores their pride and gives them schools. When they cry out in sickness and despair he hears them and builds hospitals and bridges and highways. When elected Senator and President he'll be a Leader who transforms us. Be our salvation bringing back the great American Dream forgotten by fat dumb and unhappy people who think only of their selfish ambitions. That's why his campaign is so important. A matter of life or death for our country. Can't you see that?"

Berl hesitated, overwhelmed by new and strange ideas beyond his understanding. "I was afraid," he said. "All those men with guns and dark glasses frightened me."

"Frightened?" Cora replied. "There's nothing to be scared of! You just have to trust a great Leader like my father to do what is right!"

Berl shook his head. "How can you be so sure? What if he does something wrong?"

Cora laughed and held his hand. "Boy are you dumb. You don't know anything about Politics. Do you?"

"I guess I don't," Berl replied. Unconvinced.

Berl tried to understand what was happening. After travelling with Cora several weeks he somehow seemed different with erotic dreams leaving him confused and exhausted. Cora inhabited his mind. He stared at her face and smiled enjoying her delightful laughter and when she spoke he blushed and trembled like a schoolboy. He was in love. Floating on air. Transported to another world. At night, in the darkened Bus, driving to the next campaign stop, he held her in his arms, her head pillowed on his shoulder and he felt the inexpressible joy of a lover. Nothing in life could be better than being with her. She was not a Cinderella hand Puppet but a living and breathing human being who loved him.

But then again he wondered what he becoming a part of? Being absorbed by? Distributing hand Bills to enthusiastic crowds of Hominy voters their angry voices shouting hatred and fury frightened and repelled him. Where did such anger and fear come from? What would it lead to? And what was Governor Hominy saying about British Bankers and Jews? What was he going to do when elected? And what of his dream of living free beholden to no one but his conscience? Yes! Berl wanted to live a life worth living and not merely serve another man's ambitions. And yes! Love can be the "Devil's Candy" and certainly now is the time for hard choices. Freedom or entrapment? To live a good life a man must make the right choices. Encountering life's daily miracles, Berl determined to accept the magic, power and salvation of loving, for love, he realized, made him more aware of his existence experiencing the sights and sounds and colors of the world with adolescent intensity. Banishing the confusion and fears that drove him from home Berl's transition to manhood began. The boy could now become a man who finds there are many things that cannot be easily learned and the price for such knowledge is high. Through the slightest personal experience of the spirit Berl discovered he who seeks adventure will experience it according to the measure of his courage for there is a mystery that happens whenever we are faithful to ourselves.

"Does that damn piss-ant sergeant Dante think he is the Gestapo? Like we are living in Russia or Germany where everyone spies and informs on his neighbors and friends and even his family can be compelled to testify against him. And that corrupt Judge who issued that Court Order? I can't believe what they're doing to me. My financial records are no one's business but mine. This is America! We have laws about privacy. Every man's home is his castle. I'm doing my best, meeting my fiduciary responsibility to Berl no matter what the Judge says. So I have a sloppy accountant? So the books are not so Kosher? Is that a crime? And how else could they be with that great Impresario, that thief Goldfarb robbing us blind? They should look into his records. Believe me he's some Goniff. And what's so bad? I gamble a little? I play the stock market? I win some. I lose some. That's the American way? Yes? And every month all our bills get paid. Our creditors are happy. We're not bankrupt. So what have I done wrong? To hear them talk you'd think I'm embezzling from my son with Berl sitting there in court hearing what they're saying about his father. What a shame hurting a boy that way. A father who lives only for his son. I have no life I call my own. My every thought is for my talented gifted son. Such a prodigy doesn't happen only once in a million years. Such a miracle! A boy wonder! I knew from the day he was born he was special. Different. Never just quiet like some babies in their cribs eating and sleeping and pooping day and night. Not my little Berl. I could hear him making music. Amazing sounds before he said a word. Singing. And don't I have a right to raise my son, to guide him, to show him how to live a positive and creative and productive life and not get bogged down in the filthy muck and mire of this trash-can crazy world. And when he became a celebrity, protecting Berl from the press and the critics and his adoring fans and all of life's temptations and stupidities became my full-time job. And believe me I met my responsibilities no matter what that stupid Judge says. So, tell me, is it a crime I should have a little drink every now and then?"

"Don't hit me no more Daddy! Don't hit me no more!" the boy in a dream screamed. "Don't hit me no more!" Struggling for sleep after an exhausting day's campaigning, "Bull" Hominy dreamt about his childhood, his Father punishing him with a heavy leather belt as he begged for mercy. "Don't hit me no more, Daddy! Don't hit me no more!" became a painful memory indelibly imprinted on Governor Hominy's blighted soul. Born to a "Poor White Trash" family picking cotton, plowing and sowing from sunrise to sunset, Tenant Farmers died young worn out by lives of profitless toil. Pellagra, and moonshine alcohol ended his father's short violent and illiterate life. His six children, four boys and two girls slept together on a corn- shuck mattress in a two room shack with an Outhouse and a polluted well. Always hungry, they filled their swollen bellies with turnip greens, grits and molasses while their mother endured her husband's brutal rages cooking and cleaning and struggling to feed her family. She read the Bible every day and blessed the food before every meal. "Bull" Hominy loved her.

"You can be as good a man as any," he recalled his mother advising him. "No man is trash no matter what some folks who don't know better say." Seated next to the light of a kerosene table lamp after the evening meal she found the strength to read Bible stories to her children, and, as they grew older, *Pilgrim's Progress* and "Bull's" favorite *The Life if*

Abraham Lincoln whose father was also a drunken illiterate. "You can be like honest Abe," his mother insisted, telling her favorite child "anything you want to be you can be."

"Bull" listened and learned for only his mother talked to him like he was a young man. "Life ain't easy," she advised. "Life is a hard road to travel but God will give you the strength to bear with your troubles," she said with conviction. Consoling her son, holding him in her arms for a brief tender moment, she showed him the only affection he ever received. "Pain and suffering ain't so bad if you got someone to love," she said, regretting what she had lost.

Despite his father insisting he work in the fields picking cotton like his brothers and sisters, "Bull" Hominy attended a one room schoolhouse, walking five miles a day to learn to read and write and do arithmetic. Seeing him lowering his head over textbooks as if physically confronting his ignorance, the teacher named him "Bull", a wild animal fighting illiteracy in a state where seventy per cent were illiterate. "You are different from my other students," she told him one day. "You have gumption. Get up and go! You certainly are kind of special and if you stay after class there's a whole lot of other things I can teach you." And so "Bull" Hominy stayed in his seat for several more hours each day walking home long after dark.

After another severe beating, "Bull" Hominy ran away to a nearby city where he worked as a Stevedore unloading cargoes arriving on ships from all over the world. Boxes and crates from London, Marseille, Bremen, Amsterdam, Hong Kong, Rio de

The Prodigy

Janeiro, and Buenos Aires showed him the existence
of an exotic and unknown world of possibilities and
promise. A world he would someday try to make his
own.

The city's Library became his University. A
sympathetic Librarian his mentor. Every evening
ignoring the daily aches and pains of his job, he read
until he was almost blind guided by an
understanding woman eager to satisfy a young
man's hunger to learn. He read Charles Dickens who
showed him poverty and suffering were universal.
Mark Twain taught him the value of laughter and
reading Jack London he discovered he was not alone
struggling to survive a brutal world. And to the
Librarian's delight and amazement he also mastered
Blackstone's Commentary On The Law passing the
State's Bar exam enabling him to defend poor and
miserable citizens living without hope.

Campaigning in his battered Model T Ford,
"Bull" Hominy toured familiar rural areas of
unpainted barns, Cotton Gins and Tobacco sheds
travelling a landscape as uninviting as the moon.
Wearing rolled up shirtsleeves and bib overalls he
seemed to emerge from the red clay soil he once
worked. An angry shouting "Redneck" now a
candidate for the Senate proclaiming undying hatred
of poverty and ignorance. Truly "A man of the
people", a Populist attacking the government's
failure to do anything about the misery blighting the
lives of impoverished farmers. His constituents
roared agreement when he shouted again and again:
"I'm an angry man and I won't take it anymore!
And you don't have to accept hunger and illness as a

part of your life!" He carried this message to Main street, schoolhouses, Town Fairs and Barbecues throughout the state accompanied by an affectionate daughter who provided him with glasses of cold water and a large red bandana to wipe the sweat from his brow. Politicians Legislators and journalists at the State Capitol considered him another ambitious dumb small town Lawyer. A country "Hick" with delusions of grandeur telling the poor, who will be with us always, what they wanted to hear. Underestimating his determination they had no idea of what a threat "Bull" Hominy had become to the corporate and political powers that ruled the state and city for generations.

Parking his Ford in a well-marked no parking zone in front of the State Capitol, "Bull" Hominy got out of his car carrying a Bull Horn and climbed the steps to the building's main doorway where turning and looking out over a crowd of enthusiastic supporters he smiled and waved and danced a little Jig like a triumphant warrior conquering an enemy. The delighted crowd who came to watch the fun roared. Then in a loud and reverent voice he began reading all the Articles of The Bill of Rights proclaiming them as if they were a Holy Catechism. The Police converged on "Bull" Hominy blowing whistles and shouting orders to disperse the crowd and end an unlawful demonstration. The demonstrators locked arms surrounding their candidate shouting "Freedom of Speech! Freedom of Speech! Freedom of Speech!" Pushing and shoving and using their clubs viciously, the Police handcuffed "Bull" Hominy shoving him into a Police Van and charging him with inciting a Riot.

The Prodigy

After a night in Jail, listening to his supporters chanting below his cell window, "Free "Bull" Hominy! Free "Bull" Hominy! Free "Bull" Hominy!" he was arraigned and tried the next morning, the Judge fining and scolding him saying angrily: "We've had just about enough of that Constitution stuff around here. Enough to last a lifetime."

"Yes, Sergeant Dante it is true. I fell head-over-heels in love with Berl the first time he pierced my heart with a golden arrow of delight smiling at me with innocent and trusting eyes that had never known betrayal. He was the most beautiful boy I had ever mentored. When he smiled his cheeks dimpled. With hair flowing down to his shoulders he walked in beauty right into my soul, into my very being. I was possessed. He was the most gifted of all my students becoming the meaning and purpose of my life. Thinking about his future brought tears to my eyes. I thanked God for this opportunity to guide and protect such a precious talent. Some artists are destined to work in paint or stone. I was privileged to work in flesh and blood. Minds and spirits infinite in their possibilities. A young boy's mind is Tabula Rasa. A blank unwritten page I will inscribe with the flame of my thought benefitting Berl from my lifetime of study. Oh what joy! What indescribable joy! How fortunate I am to be given such a treasure to work with. Let the ugly vultures of the music world write their prurient gossip. What do they know of such beauty? They are nothing but tone deaf savage critics unable to hear the glorious music of the human heart. Of two hearts, one young, one

50

old, beating together as one. For when Berl plays his violin the stars in the heavens smile and I am ecstatic.

And yes sergeant It is true. In a world that prefers the noise and chatter of modern life to the celestial harmonies of the universe, playing and listening to classical music is the last redoubt, the last fortress, the last buttress against insanity. Against the brutalization and dehumanization and growing insensitivity of our culture fostered by that ubiquitous monster called the media. Radios and newspapers make us forget how to cry out at the sight of human torment. How to feel for the sorrows of the unfortunate. How to recognize the humanity we all share with those who are victims of a cruel and malignant fate. And yes, it cannot be denied, Berl and I were enthralled, sharing the common fate of all who are possessed by each other. There is now a chasm of sorrow, a tormenting pain in the very depths of my being, a crying out against the cruelty of Berl's disappearance."

Rudi and Berl's Red Hot Fiddlin contests did more than gather and warm-up crowds at "Bull" Hominy's campaign stops. The two fiddlers facing each other, stamped their feet as they sawed away on their violins playing with increasing speed such patriotic spine-chilling songs as *Dixie*. The audience clapped their hands and roared approval. With a hoop and a holler and a rebel yell governor Hominy danced a two-step jig across the podium. His back straight, arms raised above his head, pounding the floor with his cowboy boots, he struggled to keep up with the music. Berl, unable to compete with Rudi's high speed fiddling, dropped out of the contest accepting defeat. Victory assured, Rudi stopped playing, triumphantly bowing to the audience and then graciously meeting their request for an encore playing several choruses of *My Little Brown Jug*. The crowd responded singing: "Yo Ho Ho, you and me, little Brown jug how I love thee" as a prelude to an evening drinking "White Lightning" and cold beer.

Berl soon acquired other tasks than fiddling with Rudi and holding hands with Cora. Governor Hominy welcomed him aboard the campaign bus from where Berl distributed campaign press releases and signed photographs, tacking posters on walls and trees, and carrying the Bull horn for the governor as smiling and laughing he worked the crowd, reaching out, shaking outstretched hands, kissing babies and enthusiastic girls and women.

Traveling to another campaign stop the Governor invited Berl to sit beside him. "When we arrive at the next town," he said, "I want you to go to the Cemetery and get me some names."

"Names?" Berl asked. Confused.

"Yes," replied the Governor. "You'll find there's a whole lot of names on the graves just waiting to be resurrected."

"Resurrected?" Berl said wondering about this unusual request.

"Yes. Resurrected. Those names ain't doing anything for anybody just sitting there on stones eroding in the wind and the rain and the weather. Signed on a Petition they can benefit the living."

"How is that possible?" Berl asked.

"A Petition, "the Governor explained patiently, "asks the Government to do something about the mess we're in. Not tomorrow or next month but right away! A thousand names is a powerful voice telling our leaders what people really want. Ten thousand names and the powers that be will really pay attention. That's why I want you to get me a whole lot of names for my Petitions."

Berl thought about this a moment and then said: "What will you be asking the government to do?"

"Well I don't rightly know today. But get me the names and tomorrow I'll think of something. Give people what they think they want and they'll vote for you forever."

"But those names are people who are dead," Berl said confused.

"That's why they're buried," the Governor said, irritated by the question. "Then how can you know what they want?"

"Believe me dead or alive all people want the same," the Governor insisted. "Food, clothing, shelter. That's all there is. There ain't much more to life than that!"

"I won't do it," Berl told Cora the next day. Shaking his head. "I can't go to a graveyard and get names for your father."

"There's nothing to be afraid of," Cora assured him. "There's nothing there can hurt you."

"I'm not afraid," Berl insisted, "I've been to cemeteries."

"Then what's your problem?" Cora asked. "Nobody will stop you from writing down names of people who died a long time ago."

"It's disrespectful. Sacrilegious." Berl replied. "I don't think they would like it."

"Who are you talking about ?" Cora asked.

"The dead," Berl answered.

Cora laughed. "They won't know anything about it," she said.

"May be so." Berl replied. "But that don't make it right."

Cora caressed Berl's hand. "You are a darling boy," she said affectionately. "Never met anyone like you before."

"It's wrong and I won't do it," Berl insisted. Cora reached out and put her arm around Berl. "My daddy needs those names to get elected. To do some good. To help people live a better life. What can be wrong about that?"

"That doesn't make it right," Berl repeated.

"How can you say that?" Cora asked. "My Daddy hasn't done anything wrong in his whole life!"

"Telling lies is wrong! Signing dead people's names who don't know what they are signing must be wrong!"

Cora removed her arm from around Berl turning to speak to him. "I think you're an ignorant little boy who doesn't know a thing about how the world really works. You're just dumb."

"Maybe so but I know a lie when I see one! I know right from wrong!" Berl shouted angrily. "And if you can't see what I see then you're really truly blind."

FOUR

Maestro Leonardo's lectures were highly valued by students at the world-famous Julliard Music school. Seated or standing at a Grand piano in front of the class he played from his vast musical memory selections from the scores of all the great composers. With his left hand fingering the keyboard, waving his right hand to emphasize his comments, his long hair swayed back and forth like a metronome keeping time to his performance. Leonardo was indeed a great teacher possessed by his subject.

Berl and Menahim were overwhelmed by Leonardo's teaching. Struggling to absorb his assault on their young and eager minds, they relieved the suffering of hour-long lectures by exchanging hopeless looks, shaking their heads at each other, while their smiles and laughter saved them from despair. Standing or seated, jumping up and down while playing the piano with one hand, Leonardo's behavior often reminded them of what they had seen at the Central Park Zoo.

Menahim was the youngest and shortest student in a class of growing adolescents who were amazed at the volume and intensity of the music coming from someone his size. Called the "Runt" or "Shorty", Menahim studied and practiced accepting the taunts of his classmates without protest. Berl considered him the most talented student at the Music school, the one with the greatest expectation of success in the highly competitive world of

classical music. Menahim sensed Berl's approval,
and as an only child, adopted Berl as the brother he
never had. One who would raise his spirits when
down, and applaud his growing mastery of the
violin. After six hours of diligent practicing isolated
in rehearsal rooms with a violin and a musical score
their only companions, they met and talked to each
other as more than classmates in a growing
friendship that soon became a deep and abiding
love.

Berl became aware of growing feelings of
affection he had never experienced before. Desires
and expectations aroused by Menahim' s smile, face
or voice. Surges of emotions Berl did not
understand. Could not identify. Could not control.
What is happening to me he wondered?

"Believe me Sergeant Dante It was a hollow
victory. One I take no pride in. A triumph I did not
enjoy. When First Prize in the prestigious Queen
Elizabeth Violin competition was awarded to me I
felt in my heart of hearts Berl would have won had
he been able to perform. Our competitive instincts
were raised by Maestro Leonardo to a level of
unbearable suffering by demanding diligent hours of
practice and study. We competed in a musical
culture where there was no alternative to being the
best and highest paid child prodigy on the concert
circuit. Leonardo's methods were diabolical giving
or withholding approval or rejection, exploiting our
childish fear of failure. Alternating anger and love,
coolness and warmth, he became our God who
would not allow us to fail. At night, at home, our
ambitious mothers would not tolerate complaints.

Listen to our pain. We were immature foot soldiers in a parental combat where in war, as in love, everything is permissible.

Berl and I were united in our love of music. We were more brothers than rivals. We completed each other. Together we were no doubt a genius. Critics rightly praised my finer more polished technique. Skills acquired through brutal hard work. Hours repeating the same difficult passages over and over again until they were mastered. But Berl had a musical voice that came from his soul. A sound I envied and could never hope to acquire for it belonged only to Berl. A living, throbbing voice echoing a thousand years of human suffering. A voice that was a gift of the Gods! How could Berl not have won First Prize?

I had trouble sleeping. Lost weight. No longer looked forward to the next concert, the next performance to audiences attracted by the prestige of my Award. There was a falsehood in the center of my life that was hard to bear. Difficult to accept. "Grow up! Snap out of it!" my mother insisted. "it's time to grow up. Be grateful for your luck." I became depressed. Could not play. Cancelled concerts.

"How can you do this to me?" my mother complained. "After all I have sacrificed for your career. Don't you know you wouldn't be where you are but for me? For what I have done for you!"

Traveling across our spacious mid-western states Berl resumed skating through the heart of America where church Steeples rising above distant horizons reached up to the sky inspiring him to continue his remarkable journey. Now for the first time in his life Berl saw the America of small towns where welcoming signs proclaimed names and populations and unique claims to fame of every village though most looked alike. Main street merchants served local residents and nearby farmers who arrived every Saturday for their weekly shopping and afternoon movie. Some elderly shoppers, fatigued by their chores, sat and relaxed under ancient Oak trees on the Town Green where in the evening musicians on the Bandstand played *America The Beautiful* and *The Battle Hymn Of The Republic*. Off in the darkening shadows on the far side of the Green, romantic young lovers embraced and kissed with an adolescent passion as old as the history of mankind.

"Now I've seen just about everything " an Old Man standing on the sidewalk said waving his hand laughing and smiling at Berl. "Roller skates!" he shouted. "Guess I've seen just about everything now." Walking to the curb where Berl had stopped to rest he asked: "Where you from, Mars?"

"New York," Berl replied.

"New York! Never been there and don't expect I ever will," the Old Man said. Then carefully studying Berl and liking what he saw asked: "If you're in need of a good meal and a warm bed for the night you've come to the right place."

"Thank you," Berl replied. "I'd appreciate that."

"Well you more than welcome, son. It's not every day I get to talk to a roller skater."

That evening, at the dinner table, as the father and mother led their children blessing their food, Berl witnessed the joys of family life. Asked about his family he never mentioned travelling the world dining alone in expensive restaurants with only a book or musical score for company.

Skating over our rolling Prairie lands Berl arrived one evening at a small isolated village with only a few homes, a narrow Main street, General Store, Post Office, and a tall Grain Silo set amidst an ocean of wheat fields. Seated in a rocking chair on the porch of his house, a bearded old Farmer in bib overalls wearing a straw hat rose from his chair and walked to the roadside where Berl stopped to tighten a skate. Staring at Berl's feet the old Farmer shook his head saying: "If you haven't got wings I expect roller skates will get you wherever you're going."

"Faster than walking," Berl replied.

"I suppose so. That's probably why they were invented. There's no limit to what people can think of these days." Then, considering this thought a moment he asked: "Is skating hard to do?"

"No."

"Someday maybe I'll learn to skate. Probably break my neck. But then again a man should try everything at least once before he dies."

"I guess so," Berl replied and turned to continue skating.

"Do you know where you're going?" the Old Farmer asked.

"I think I do."

"It's important a young man knows where he's going with his life. Must have a destination. A plan. Otherwise he just wandering all by himself in darkness."

"Well I don't mind travelling alone meeting all kinds of interesting people."

"I'm glad to hear that. People are important. Meeting all kinds helps you grow up. Still there's no need for you go through life all by yourself. Traveling alone as if you don't have a friend in the world."

"I expect I'll make friends where I'm going."

"Where's that?"

"California."

"The Promised Land," the Old Farmer replied. "So you're another Pilgrim fleeing to the Golden State of sunshine and dreams."

"I guess so," Berl said.

"You have a long lonesome road ahead of you son, believe me when I say there's no need for you to travel that road all by yourself. You'll never walk alone if you have someone by your side."

"Who is that?" Berl asked.

"God!" the Old Farmer replied. "You'll never walk alone as long as God is at your side." He then turned and watching the sun set looked down at his watch. Then smiling at Berl he said: "It's Friday evening. Why don't you take off your skates and come and join me and my family welcoming the Sabbath? You look like a good meal and a warm bed for the night would be a blessing. A Mitzvah."

This dinner table was different from others Berl had been invited to. Bright freshly washed children sat patiently waiting for the evening meal to begin. The Old Farmer wearing his best suit, his grey beard carefully combed, presided over the ritual like a Prince or a King. With a slow graceful movement the mother struck a match and reached out to light two tall candles, her head bowed, her hands covering her face as she welcomed the gift of another Sabbath. Then the Old Farmer, in a soft almost sing-song voice blessed the food they were about to eat and the good sweet world in which they lived.

Then, turning to Berl, he handed him a prayer book. "Would you like to read the Shema?" he asked.

Berl shook his head. "I can't read Hebrew."

Surprised, the Old Farmer asked: "How old are you?"

"Fifteen," Berl replied, humiliated by his ignorance. "Weren't you Bar Mitzvahed?" the Old Farmer asked.

"No," Berl replied. Embarrassed. Shamed.

"I'm sorry to hear that," the Old Farmer said sadly as if the evening's joy had been diminished.

"My parents didn't believe in Bar Mitzvahs. They said religion was the Opium of the People."

"My poor boy," the Old Farmer said. "Is that what they taught you?"

"But I've been Baptized," Berl explained. Hopefully. "Blessed in the blood of the Lamb."

"Baptized?" said the Old Farmer. "Blessed in Dreck! " he shouted angrily. Then suddenly calm. His anger subsiding he continued: "Now I know there have always been Jews, to save their lives, or get on with their careers have been Baptized. But you? You're a young boy just starting out in life naked as the day you were born."

"But I'm really a Jew," Berl insisted.

"Are you?" the Old Farmer asked. "You have no idea of what it is to be a Jew. It's not so easy being Jewish."

"Why is that?" Berl asked.

"Because a Jew is always asking questions. Always arguing. Never knows a moment of peace."

"What's so bad about that?" Berl asked.

"Bad?" the Old Farmer shouted. "It can be a living hell! Morning noon and night a Pious Jew asks himself: What kind of Jew am I? What kind of Jew have I been? Did I show compassion? Hate violence? Been gentle, kind and modest? Was I concerned for the suffering of others? Did I have the courage to do what I thought right and just despite being hated, scorned and detested? I tell you it's asking too much! Too many questions! Such thoughts can drive a God-fearing Jew mad!"

"Well I'm certainly glad you came to see me Sergeant," said Ziggy Goldfarb the great Impresario, President of Goldfarb Entertainment. "I've had a lot on my mind and no one to talk to. Lost a lot of sleep worrying about Berl." He reached out opening a humidor on his desk. "Do you smoke," he asked. "These are Cuban," he continued, offering Dante one. "Upman Amitista the world's finest cigar."

"No thank you," Dante replied. "I've stopped. Doctor's orders."

"Too bad. I hope it's nothing serious."

"No. The say six packs a day is a death sentence."

"May be so, may be so," Goldfarb replied selecting a cigar and lighting it. He leaned back in his high-backed executive chair and blew a perfect smoke ring across the desk. "If you've come to ask me about that law suit there's not much I can say. We're still litigating and I'm not allowed to speak without a lawyer present."

"I don't really understand Berl. I'm told you knew him."

"True. True. He was like a son. The one I never had. A boy whose parents had a lot to learn about raising a child. His mother was a headache. My most difficult client. A nonstop complainer. An unhappy Diva with limited talent."

"His parents seemed devoted to him."

"Devoted?" Goldfarb said. "Yes indeed. Devoted to making money. Greedy. I built Berl's career. All the major concert halls in the world were begging for him to come and play. He was a bigger attraction than the Russian Ballet. And now they say I screwed them. Inflated my expenses. Kept money that was theirs. And a whole lot of other bull shit my lawyer says the Judge will dismiss with prejudice. And in the middle of all this is a lonely hungry child. Hungry for affection, not really understanding what's going on. As far I'm concerned his parents should drop dead."

"My Country Tis of thee sweet land of liberty of thee I sing!" For the first time in his life Berl felt a patriotic and overwhelming love of country. "Land of our father's pride, home where the Pilgrims died" were now more than words. Skating across Montana's grazing lands, under the big sky of the American west, Berl enjoyed an intoxicating freedom. He was voyaging through an endless sea of prairie grass extending out to the horizon where

The Prodigy

every evening distant mountain ranges reflecting the setting sun gave each day its moment of glory. He was travelling a land where people welcomed strangers without question. Hospitality was a habit in a region where miles separated isolated farmhouses from their neighbors. At every truck stop or campsite he was offered food and friendship and invitations to ride with lonely travelers hoping to find someone to share the driving. Unable to skate in high winds, or rain Berl often accepted with each traveler giving him a greater understanding of the common decency of his countrymen. He became proud to be an American.

Berl said yes to a tall, friendly traveler who after buying him a cup of coffee and pointing at the approaching storm clouds asked if he wanted a ride. The traveler explained he never refused good honest American Hitchhikers seeking a better life, helpless victims of powers beyond their control, victims of the great depression.

Sitting behind the steering wheel as they drove along the highway, Berl watched the traveler lean forward in his seat and reach out to turn on the car radio. A chorus of Gospel singers filled the car with glorious music. "Now isn't that wonderful," the traveler said, clapping his hands in time to the music, shouting a joyful "Amen" to each chorus. "Radio is the greatest invention since sliced white bread," the traveler said. "Wouldn't own a car without a radio," he explained. "A salesman's life away from home is a whole lot easier with something to listen to."

"What are you selling?" Berl asked.

"Bibles," the traveler replied. "The good book! Greatest book ever written. Millions of copies been sold around the world. The book that changed the world!"

Berl shifted gears as the car approached an upgrade in the highway. He nodded, thinking about what he had just been told. "My territory is from St. Louis to the Rockies and that's a lot of driving seeing customers and it ain't much fun no matter what they say about travelling salesmen and the farmer's daughter."

"I never read the Bible," Berl said. "We didn't have one at home."

"Well, we'll do something about that," the traveler replied. "I'll give you a Bible free of charge and you'll learn everything you need to know about living a good life from the Bible. Nothing better than the Bible to guide you through all the evil in this world. Better than reading a newspaper or listening to the radio although you can learn a whole lot from the radio. Radio helps you keep up with the news. Know who is not worth a damn and who is important. Like Henry Ford who paid five dollars a day so his workers could buy his cars. And that's why I only drive Fords and what's more he's for keeping us out of another war that's supposed to make America safe for democracy. He and Lucky Lindy know what they're talking about. Makes no sense getting killed for the British and the Jewish Bankers. And every Sunday there's Father Coughlin on the radio telling how Wall street and the Communists are destroying America. How greedy corporations and money changers are the great Satan doing the devil's work. He has thirty million listeners. Gets more mail than President Franklin D. Rosenfeld. It's an education listening to him tell how Capitalism robs labor of their fair share of what they produce. And how he'll keep on fighting for guaranteed work and income for everybody. And how the Supreme Court now only protects the rights of the rich and not the poor. And how this country is being taxed out of existence. He's all for sending the Jews back from where they come from in a slow and leaky boat. Seems to me like Father Coughlin just can't wait until Hitler comes here and shows us how to run a country."

"Hitler? Who is Hitler?" Berl asked.

The traveler stared at Berl a moment. "Never heard of Hitler?"

"No."

"Ever listen to the radio?"

"No."

"Read a newspaper?" Berl shook his head. Embarrassed by the questions.

"Where you been all your life" the traveler asked. "How you going to know what's going on in the world if you don't listen to the radio or read a newspaper? How you going to know what to think?"

Berl said nothing. Concentrating on driving.

"Hitler," the traveler explained. "Is a great Leader. Germany was in worse shape than we are today and he saved Germany from the communists about to destroy their country. He's the kind of great Leader we need to save America by driving the money-changers out of the temple!"

Sergeant Emiliano hated songs insulting the heroism of Italian Draftees during the first World

War. His most vivid childhood memories were the glorious sound of opera recordings performed by the great Enrico Caruso. The musical God of New York City's "Little Italy". Certainly Dante's father Giovanni enjoyed listening to Caruso more than working as a garbage collector supporting a large and boisterous family. Children's stories like *Snow White*, *Pinocchio*, or *Little Bo Peep* were unknown to Dante. Instead, as Caruso's powerful voice filled their two room cold water flat with arias of passion, joy, and heart-breaking love, Sergeant Dante acquired an astounding memory of Librettos and often felt his life was another Grand Opera. Giovanni who believed singing is man's way of merging with God enjoyed telling the stories to his son, often performing his favorite roles in a strong passionate though untrained voice. Dante applauded enthusiastically as his father's sang Tonio the Clown's prologue to *Pagliacci*. While working at the Bureau Dante recalled his father standing erect, opening his arms, his head back, mouth open singing in a sonorous voice: "What you are about to see is a true story showing that actors and clowns have the same joys and sorrows as other people."

Sergeant Dante tacked this statement on the wall in front of his desk to help him understand the actors, clowns, musicians and flamboyant Impresarios he dealt with every day. A parade of dramatic characters like Canio whose wife was seduced by Silvio in a story of jealousy, betrayal, revenge and murder. In a rage Canio stabbed his wife and killed her lover singing "Vesti La Giubba. On with the show!"

The Prodigy

"Finding a missing person is no laughing matter" Dante shouted aloud as other Agents in the office turned to stare at him wondering if he was sober. "A fucking tragedy of clowns, liars and drunks," he said, lowering his voice. "Berl's disappearance is no play, no three-act comedy, no make-believe performance on a stage or screen. It's God damn real and I'm not even close to that moment in the story when the curtain comes down and the Clown announces to the audience: "La Comedia es Finita! This Comedy is finished!"

Berl did not understand what he was seeing. Skating on a lonely road crossing the high plains country of the far west he arrived at a small abandoned village now mounds of rubble. A church steeple rising above ruins that were once homes of a thriving community swayed in the wind threatening to fall. An overturned wreck of a car was parked on the roof of a home without walls or windows. Uprooted trees blocked both sides of the road. In what had once been Main street a battered piano waited for ghost musicians to arrive and sit down and play. Chairs, tables and empty beds and a bathtub filled with rainwater were remaining evidence of vanished lives. Berl stopped for a moment to stare at the disaster wondering where were all the people? Did anyone survive? Can life be this fragile? Alive and happy one moment. And then, suddenly, without warning, disappear?

As if answering his question, Berl saw on the distant horizon an approaching wall of black threatening clouds accompanied by flashing streaks of lightning and the menacing rumble of thunder.

Headwinds he had been skating against reversed direction. A powerful hand pushed him towards rotating spirals, whirlwinds reaching down to the ground like the descending finger of malevolent Fate. Terrified, unable to stand, breathing laboriously, Berl lay flat on the ground shielding his head with his hands convinced he was about to die. "Oh no! Oh no!" he shouted as dirt and rubble covered him like a burial shroud. Berl trembled and cried and thought about the cruelty of his misfortune to be at the wrong place at the wrong time. "So this is what it is like to die," he said to himself.

Then a hand grabbed his leg pulling him over the ground, dragging his body over the rough rubble. Slowly, by a force he did not understand, Berl felt himself moved towards an unknown destination and he cried out for help sobbing: "My God! My God!" before he lost consciousness.

Berl awoke in a large storm shelter illuminated by a flickering kerosene lamp. Seated on a bench along one wall an old man offered him a canteen of water. He leaned over Berl saying: "Here, drink all you want. But slow and easy." Berl sat up, raised the canteen to his mouth, and when revived, looked around the shelter. "You're in a cyclone cellar," the old man explained. "We got rations, water, blankets all the comforts of home." Berl took another drink, nodded and turned to the old man. "Thanks for saving my life." The old man laughed. "Think nothing of it. Glad to help a Pilgrim in distress."

"Where is everybody?" Berl asked, "Don't know. Warned them about what's coming. You know. Armageddon. Get underground I told them.

But nobody listens to an old man. Now they're God knows where."

"You the only survivor?"

"That's me all right! Last man standing. Got no other place to go. Born and raised right here. Wouldn't think of living anywhere else."

"But it's all gone," Berl said.

The old man laughed. "Not as long as I'm still alive and well and saluting the flag every morning." He pointed at an American flag on the shelter's back wall. "That's Old Glory! The stars and stripes will live forever!" Berl had another drink, put down the canteen and looked around the shelter noticing something he had never seen before. "That's an old wind-up Victrola. A record player," the old man explained. "Seeing how we got no electricity an old wind-up is all we have. You like music?" Berl nodded. "What would you like to hear? I saved all my records. Every one of them. Life ain't worth living without music." Berl remained silent. "I have my favorites," the old man said. "There's some music I just can't get enough of." He turned the crank on the Victrola winding up the spring. Searching through a stack of records he placed one on the turntable. "This record cheers me up when I'm down," he said before lowering the needle on the record and turning on the player.

"Music enables you to defeat loneliness. Tells you how to be truly alive. To be grateful for the gift of life!"

The glorious opening chords of Beethoven's *Ode To Joy* filled the shelter as Berl, overwhelmed with feeling, covered his face with his hands, fighting back tears as he sobbed and all the old misery emptied from his young, wandering heart.

FIVE

Paradise Lodge Rehab is a second home to Celebrities seeking respite from lives of alcohol, drugs and desperate dissipation. Photographs of famous stage and screen stars decorated the walls. Thick carpets quiet the floors creating an atmosphere of therapeutic tranquility. The Staff never raise their voices. Loudspeakers never attack the silence. Telephone and Call bells are muted. Neither radio or newspapers disturb patients with news of the outside world. Paradise Lodge provided a guaranteed escape from the hectic blaring noise, the endless "Buzz" of a world gone mad.

Paradise Lodge's Founder and Director, Doctor Franz Frankel is proud of his ability to rehabilitate, restore, and reenergize patients in despair at what they have done to their lives. He achieves amazing recoveries from attempted suicides by calling on the secret strength contained in depression to evoke the resilience that restores balance in the human psyche. His photograph on one widely circulated magazine cover was headlined: "The Doctor who revives the hopeless."

Sergeant Dante's surveillance of Menahim, winner of the most prestigious International violin competition led him to Paradise Lodge when he learned the boy Prodigy was Dr. Frankle's patient. Tall, elegant and charming, speaking in a soft voice Dr. Frankel answered Sergeant Dante's question with a moment of hesitation.

"Patient confidentiality limits what I can say, Sergeant."

Dante nodded explaining his request was unofficial. "I can't add much to what's in the press," Dr. Frankle replied. "A shameless sewer of gossip and misinformation."

"Celebrity news sells papers, Doctor Frankle."

"Yes. And there are no private lives anymore. Just private pain patients must suffer alone," Dr. Frankle replied. "Menahim agonized over events he could not understand. He was in despair. Performing was a torment he could no longer endure."

"Was his overdose deliberate?"

"Accidental or deliberate can never be determined. We do know he became totally dysfunctional feeling pain he could not control. Living with pain dissolves our coherence. He fell apart and now we're trying to help him pick up the pieces of his life and resume his career."

"And your prognosis?"

"Unfortunately not good. There is an obstacle to his recovery that appears intractable."

"And what is that?"

"Menahim's mother. Dear old Mom. Not a loving mother. Children must think of their mother's as perfect. Mother has to be wise and kind and when something happens to shatter that belief children become angry and turn that anger back against themselves. Which is what Menahim has done. Children want to perpetuate the illusion they have a good mother. Something Menahim is now unable to do."

"What destroyed Menahim's belief in his mother?"

The Prodigy

"We don't know. His mother has been uncooperative. Refused to participate in her son's therapy. Doesn't answer our requests for information. Never returns phone calls. As far as I know she has disappeared. Vanished."

When Berl awoke this morning he began coughing to expel dust from his lungs. His sleeping bag was covered with a blanket of fine brown particles that once were the fertile topsoil of the western plains. His mouth tasted of dirt and despair and when he drank from the canteen and spit out a mouthful of water, the dust taste remained in his throat and bronchi. Skating was hard work. His labored breathing was intensified by violent winds blowing down the slopes of the Rockies forming high black walls of dust moving across once prosperous farmlands darkening skies and burying homes and entire villages. As parched sunbaked soil smoldered in the heat, the air became heavy with doom. Jack-rabbits and prairie dogs fled to their burrows. Crows and vultures were silent as if awaiting the arrival of a disaster.

Berl stopped skating, turned his back to the wind, blinded by the storm's transformation of day into night. A black fearful night. Disoriented, Berl crawled on his hands and knees to the roadside, struggling for breath, covering his face and eyes with a bandana, seeking shelter from the dust storm. An old abandoned automobile in a ditch on the side of the road became his sanctuary. Berl opened the door and crawled inside and exhausted, immediately fell asleep. A long hard sleep inhabited by strange dreams. He saw himself hiking a narrow trail up a mountain. A steep trail that seemed endless. As he struggled to climb higher each breath became an agony. Every upward step a hard-won victory fighting the pain in his trembling legs. Dark clouds obscured the trail ahead as he continued climbing. Blind. Fatigued. Forcing himself to walk and breathe, sobbing as he counted steps feeling the sorrow of a motherless child. The clouds never parted. He continued climbing with no redeeming light at the end of his tortured journey.

He awoke in the dark. No light could be seen through the dust covered windows of his buried refuge. The storm passed on. All was silent. Berl sat up believing he was trapped. No one would ever find him. This abandoned car was his tomb. With the windows sealed how much longer could he live? When would he breathe his last breath of the air remaining in his shelter? He lay down, closed his eyes and silently waited for death to end his suffering.

Instead of approaching death Berl heard voices shouting. And now he was not dreaming as he heard shovels frantically working to uncover the car. When the first rays of sunlight dispelled the darkness in the car he looked up and saw a face peering at him through a window. A face that turned away and shouted: "There's someone in there!" The shoveling continued. The door opened and Berl crawled out on to the highway standing up to thank his saviors. Two men and their wives and children silently stared at Berl as if seeing an apparition. One man held a Jerry-can of gasoline in his hand. "We ran out of gas," he explained. "That's why we left our car." The men resumed shoveling slowly uncovering their car. Berl walked up from the ditch on to the road where an old model A Ford pick-up truck was parked. Under a canvas canopy over the open back of the truck, a frail old woman covered by a heavy blanket, her head propped up on a pillow stared at Berl saying: "Looks to me like you been born again." She laughed, shook her head. Wondering aloud. "Seems to me God moves in mysterious ways there's no doubt about that!"

Berl nodded. Smiled at the old woman and walked to a large truck loaded with old furniture, a rocking chair, farming tools and bags of clothing and other family possessions secured under a large canvas tarp. They were part of a convoy of ninety thousand Farm families fleeing the devastation of the Dust Bowl when their land was blown away creating an American Exodus travelling to the promised land of California.

The family made room for Berl in the truck. He traveled with them for days slowly regaining his strength. At night, on the road side, they sat around a small campfire sharing their impoverished meal with him. Bowing their heads and giving thanks for the food before them, they fed the children and grand children first. Then the Grand parents, the parents and then Berl. All ate slowly, silently as the mother filled their bowls. Berl became aware of the bonds of family love uniting them despite their extreme poverty endured with dignity and grace. He suddenly felt his own pain of loss. Of being bereft recognizing what he had been missing all his life. What he fled from. What he hungered for. He knew then he would never return to feeling like a motherless child. His past would not be prologue to his future. His past would be nothing but an unhappy history filed away and forgotten. Two hands reached out to hold his hands and include him in the family circle around the campfire. Raising their voices, singing, almost pleading, the family sang in loud clear voices: "Rock of Ages, abide by me. Let me hide myself in thee!" Berl opened his mouth and with renewed strength and determination, tears clouding his eyes, a powerful surge of emotion rose up from the depths of his soul as he shouted "Yes! Yes! Yes! Please God! Abide by me! Abide by me!"

Following "Persons of Interest" undetected was a skill Sergeant Dante perfected after years as a Detective. Pausing at store windows or waiting in doorways, he maintained his distance behind his quarry. He considered Menahim's mother Miriam a difficult "Tail" as she stopped to enjoy New York's most expensive department stores. Sachs Fifth Avenue, Bonwit Teller, and Lord and Taylor were stations on her journey down an avenue of conspicuous consumption where high fashion and exorbitant prices were the attraction. Holidays crowds made surveillance difficult. Often impossible. Unable to follow Miriam when she entered a store, Dante would wait outside for her to reappear. A tedious job Sergeant Dante loathed. Where Miriam shopped and what she bought combined with telephone "Taps" and mail intercepts created a portrait of an elusive woman who often disappeared. Sometimes vanished without a clue. Most surprising was Miriam's successful evasions of surveillance. Flagging down a Taxi, riding a few blocks and then changing cabs, disappearing into a subway, entering and suddenly exiting as the train left the station never failed to lose Dante. A game she played with apparent delight. Where did she acquire these skills? Dante wondered. Who was she? What was her past? With no visible means of support other than Menahim, a Russian Émigré living like a Ghost without friends, family, lovers or husband, Miriam was uncooperative, did not return phone calls, simply vanished. Is she still alive? Dante wondered when discovering her history of suicidal depression. Does she still exist?

When Adults are unable to cope with unhappy love affairs, failed careers, financial or medical disasters, or paralyzing guilt, they become desperate and disappear abandoning their former identity for one that is new and shameless. Finding adults who do not want to be found is often impossible. Sergeant Dante hated failure. Admitting defeat, marking a Case "Closed" was always painful. And no doubt when Menahim leaves Paradise Lodge he will need his mother.

Sergeant Dante awoke with a start. His darkened hotel room was warm and close, smelling of dust and unwashed linen. The hard pillow under his head added to his discomfort. He never slept well away from home and disliked hotels. Travelling to investigate leads tried his patience and drained his energy. He lay still for a moment, disoriented, feeling old and exhausted. Then he sat up and watched the morning light glaring through a window that looked as if it had not been washed for years. What time is it? he wondered as he swung his legs over the side of the bed and groped the floor with his bare feet searching for shoes. He dressed quickly, glanced at his watch, and rode the elevator down to breakfast. He had time for a decent meal before meeting with an informant, a Tent Show attraction living at this hotel. After breakfast he returned to his room and dialed her room aware she may be another false lead. Posting a reward for information about Berl's disappearance overwhelmed the Bureau with a flood of telephone calls, postcards and illiterate letters that Dante had to evaluate finding only a few promising, most a waste of time. He often learned more standing on his head.

The phone rang several times before a voice endowed with beauty and deep feeling answered. A voice stirring Dante's music-loving heart evoking old memories of the great Divas he heard as a child. A voice that could make a strong man surrender his soul said: "Please come up."

He rode the elevator to her floor and knocked on the door and was greeted by that same beautiful voice: "One moment please." He waited patiently while security chains were unhooked and locks opened the voice apologizing for the delay. A large magnified eye peered at Dante through the glass peep hole. "Sergeant Dante?" the voice asked. "You are Sergeant Dante?" she repeated, concerned. Reassured, she opened the door slowly revealing her large body blocking the hallway. Sergeant Dante entered the apartment as the Fat Lady locked the door. He followed her as she walked to a large divan in the middle of the room and sat down reclining on a combined couch and bed. Publicity posters announcing her appearances at State Fairs decorated the walls. Then she smiled, her eyes bright with happy expectation. Dante felt he was looking at the face of a beautiful child trapped in an enormous body. "I read Variety every week," she said. "Couldn't live not knowing where all my friends are working, who's still alive, and who has gone to their maker. Aren't many doing Specialty Acts anymore. Freaks aren't as popular as they used to be. Show business is always changing. We are not so welcome at State Fairs now a days. Why that is I don't rightly know. People are so unpredictable. And when I read about a reward for finding that boy violinist I knew Berl was not just a country Fiddler like Rudi. That little boy could really play. Made me cry. A beautiful child. Filled with love. He just adored my Cinderella as if she was real. Fell head over heels in love. Broke his heart when he found out she was only a hand Puppet. So one morning he put on his roller skates and headed West. Gone to California I think. We all miss him. He was so normal. So like what we all would want to be. It's not so easy being different. More sensitive. Hurting more than ordinary people. I have such deep feelings, you know. Such dreams like one day I am thin and walk into a department store and try on all those pretty dresses and fancy hats and shoes. I laugh and cry even though people say I'm a Freak. A terrible word because aren't we human beings like everyone? There's something ugly in normal people. Something I'll never understand. Maybe you can figure it out. Maybe you can tell me why the Bearded lady is more popular than I am?"

Rudi The Red Hot Fiddler was also a "Deadbeat Dad" evading Bill Collectors trying to compel him to meet his financial responsibilities to his wives and children scattered like human seeds across six western states. Ignoring Court Orders and persistent Process Servers, Rudi justified his behavior saying: "Alimony is a screwing you get for a screwing you got." Constantly traveling for Governor Hominy's political campaign made Rudi hard to find. With no address, no permanent residence, home was where he parked his Hearse at night. When performing, Rudi always searched for inquisitive faces in the crowd like seeing a man loitering in back of the audience, trying to appear ordinary, turning away from the stage as if uninterested in fiddling. Someone who didn't look like a "Good Old Country Boy" chewing and spitting tobacco at a State Fair. That kind of man's name is "Trouble", Rudi decided. Real trouble.

Looking in the rear-view mirror while driving his hearse, Rudi noticed a small gray car maintaining a constant distance behind him. Whenever he turned a corner the car followed and Rudi evaded this unknown stalker knowing he would sooner or later be confronted in a game called catch me if you can. Time to move on to the next town, the next state fair, Rudi decided, and leaving Governor Hominy's campaign he would miss Cora who reminded him of his daughter.

Rudi drove into the parking lot of a local diner for lunch. Evading a "Tail" made him hungry. Hot coffee and a plate of bacon and eggs would calm his fears. Sergeant Dante entered the diner and without asking permission sat at Rudi's table. He smiled showing his credentials. "I enjoyed your playing," Dante said. "We don't have Fiddling in New York."

"So you're a Policeman?" Rudi asked, relieved.

"A Detective with the Missing Persons Bureau."

"What in hell are you doing out here in God's Country?" Rudi asked. "You come to disturb the Peace?"

"I'm here to do more than enjoy the scenery," Dante explained. "I saw you stalking me," Rudi replied. "Thought you were a Process Server or Bill Collector. How did you find me?"

"Cinderella," Dante replied. "Cinderella told me where you where."

"Cinderella?" Rudi laughed. "Now isn't that just like her. A great old Trouper if ever there was one. She had a heart as big as a whale. Everybody loves her."

Sergeant Dante reached into his pocket and pulled out a photograph. "What do you know about this boy?" Dante demanded.

"Why do you want to know?" Rudi asked.

"There's a twenty-five thousand dollar reward for information about him."

"Twenty-five thousand dollars?" Rudi said, shaking his head. "He sure must be someone important."

"He is to some people."

"Twenty-five thousand dollars, You say? That's a hell of a lot of money."

"You knew him," Dante continued.

"I sure do. He was the hottest Red Hot Fiddler I ever competed against. Like we was both on fire sawing away on the strings like we was out of our minds. People just went crazy listening to us play, stamping their feet and clapping their hands and hollering like they went insane. I tell you when we finished playing I was exhausted, never so tired in all my life just trying to keep up with him. He was a wonder no doubt about that."

"Do you know where he is?" Dante asked.

Rudi shook his head. " I wish I did cause I sure do miss that boy. He was really red hot. He fell in love with the Governor's daughter until one day they had what you might call a lover's quarrel and he just took off without a thank you or good by."

"Do you have any idea where he went?" Dante asked.

"Well he was going to California when I gave him a ride."

"California?" Dante said, "California?"

"That's what he said," Rudi insisted. "He was roller skating all the way to California. And when he saw the Governor's daughter he stayed awhile fiddling. Fiddled like a mad man, like a lost body searching for his soul. A boy trying to grow up and find himself."

"And where do think that would be?" Dante asked.

"Well If I knew I certainly would tell you. Twenty-five thousand dollars is more than I've made in a lifetime Red Hot Fiddlin. Give me that reward I'd probably go to California myself.

At Barstow, Dust Bowl Migrants turned off US Highway to enter California's lush San Joaquin valley searching for work on large industrial farms operated by profitable corporations hiring "Stoop Laborers" and "Ladder Men" to harvest America's fertile "Salad Bowl". Arriving at their Promised Land, Refugees discovered wages were thirty cents

The Prodigy

an hour for a sixteen hour day seven days a week. Sleeping in cars or irrigation ditches, hungry and ill, they competed for jobs with Mexican "wet-backs" who were allowed to cross the Border to follow the seasonally ripening crops before being annually deported. With seven thousand American Migrants arriving every month, hostile local officials formed "Bums Blockades" enforced by Vigilantes determined to return them to Arizona who accused their neighbors of dumping "Hoboes" across the State line. Agriculture and Health Inspectors and State Policemen obstructed this Exodus of the unfortunate by diligently searching their cars and trucks for plant and animal diseases that must be prevented from infecting California's highly profitable agriculture. That many of the "Okies" were hungry and ill was ignored. Denied medical care by local hospitals, or schooling for their children, aroused by politicians declaring the "Trail of Tears" from the Dust Bowl "Communist inspired", many heartless farmers, to discourage more migrants, burned surplus food crops rather than feed starving families.

With "The Golden Rule" suspended, many God fearing citizens of California were not their "Brothers Keepers". Their "American Dream" was not shared with strangers but belonged to those who arrived first. A Truth we must not deny in our ubiquitous culture of mendacity. Showing compassion for the poor, the old, the infirm, the uneducated, and the unfortunate strengthens the decency we must live by without which we most surely will perish as a nation. We are not another ancient civilization doomed to rise and fall, burned

84

into oblivion by our frailty. We are not helpless. Leading a long line of battered trucks and cars in a convoy of the destitute, Berl drove Route-66 crossing an arid wasteland where mesquite, spiked cactus, tumble weeds and Joshua trees struggled to survive perpetual drought. Only scorpions, rattlesnakes and prairie dogs inhabited the great American desert where day time heat and frigid nights endangered travelers traversing this hostile barrier to California, the land of their hopes and dreams. During the decade called "The Dirty Thirties", farmers plowing dry prairie topsoil made dust storms and half a million homeless causing a human disaster in three southwestern states. Berl heard more about this tragedy from Granny, the invalid woman reclining on a mattress in the back of his truck. Years old, she was the Matriarch of a family fleeing black blizzards of dust darkening the sky and burying their foreclosed farm. Camping on roadsides at night they sheltered from the cold and wind in tattered canvas tents that provided little rest. A large iron pot simmering over a small fire cooked the daily meal of cabbage, beans and potatoes. A canvas water bag relieved thirst in carefully measured portions while starving infants suckled from their mothers' desiccated breasts.

Welcomed by the family Berl shared the driving and daily chores, making campsites every evening when he brought Granny her meals and listened to her stories about what caused their tragic journey. "It all happened when the government gave land to build the railroads!" she said sadly. "And when the tracks went from the Mississippi to the Rocky Mountains they brought tens of thousands of

Homesteaders who for the first time in their lives could own land by just living on it." Raising a corn cob pipe to her mouth, exhaling a small puff of smoke she paused a moment before saying: "640 acres for each and every man to farm and raise a family. For three generations we plowed this thin dry topsoil God intended for grazing sheep and cattle." The old lady hesitated, arousing painful memories. "We broke the prairie with our iron plows and year after year we destroyed the great gift we had been given on this promised land." She paused to relight her pipe before continuing. "And when the war made the price of a bushel of wheat go sky high, we were overcome by greed planting winter and summer, becoming victims of our ignorance and avarice. Yes indeed! What the Good Book says is true! What the Gods would destroy they first make mad! We mortgaged our homes to buy tractors and threshers and combines. As the price of wheat went higher and higher we doubled and tripled what we were harvesting from mother earth. We became thieves, not stewards of our land convinced our good fortune would never end. And now we are forced to leave our homes where we can not see the sun at noon, where skies are black and my children and grand children can not breathe the air we polluted by failing to love and respect God's great good bounty."

Evening meals became an enjoyable daily ritual for Berl watching the family pray, head bowed, rising above their circumstances as they found renewed strength enabling them to continue their journey. They laughed, argued and talked to each other at night for they were unable to speak above the engine's roar during the day. At the back of the tent, Maria, and Joseph her husband sat together holding hands, silently watching the family eat and talk. A thin cotton dress barely covered Maria's pregnancy. Berl was moved by her beautiful face glowing with the joy of expectant motherhood. He envied Joseph. Certainly becoming a father was life's most extraordinary experience for a man.

One evening, Maria and Joe did not appear for the evening meal. Grandpa and the children and grand children sat around the cook pot silently waiting for food. Troubled by their absence, Berl walked outside to look up at the stars. In the clear desert air the Constellations revolved across the sky, a million points of light reminding him of his insignificance. He was only a small footprint on the sands of time. And so was this good suffering family he was travelling with. Then in a small canvas lean-to shelter erected against the side of the truck he saw two figures obscured in the shadows. He stepped closer, silently watching them, unaware of what he was witnessing. Joseph seated on a mattress, his back against the side of the truck, legs spread apart, arms opened wide embracing Maria who reclined back against him groaning softly in the labor pains of childbirth. Two bodies joined as one, Joe whispering endearments as Maria groaned and called out to God her voice rising from a shout to a shriek to an agonized scream. Granny kneeled on the ground between Maria's legs, saying "push harder! push harder!" reaching out with her hands to help the baby emerge with each contraction. Then, with a triumphant shout of joy, Granny held up the baby saying "it's a boy child, a boy child" as the newborn's first cry evoked shouts of joy from the family waiting anxiously in the tent.

So this was how life begins, Berl thought. Pain. Suffering. Followed by the exaltation of seeing a new life arrive, caught in the hands of God.

SIX

Lights Flashing. Sirens blaring. Motorcycles roaring. Brass Bands playing. Flags waving. Drums beating. Crowds cheering. Sergeant Emiliano Dante never saw anything more stirring than the arrival of "Bull" Hominy's campaign bus. Like the coming of a Christ, arms outstretched as if nailed to a cross, the Governor stepped out of the bus and plunged into the crowd to shake hands with eager worshippers. A fraud if ever there was one, Dante thought. Yet voters do love a demagogue. They really love him. And this Corn Pone politician can now provide promising information about Berl. A lead worth pursuing. What seemed strange in a small peaceful American town, were the motorcycle "Rough Riders", Storm Troopers in black leather breeches, boots and jackets, wearing dark sunglasses and helmets, Colt 45's holstered on their belts. There was something threatening and un-American about this campaign show, Dante thought. Like what's seen in Newsreels. A short fat Duce and a hysterical Dictator with a little mustache and upraised arm. There seemed to be fear, a contagion of dread in the air Hominy's followers breathed. Despite all their laughter and cheering, they were a mob afraid of what only their Savior can protect them. Hominy was selling fear of the future. Unremitting paralyzing fear that can make a nation abandon traditional values in what they believe was a fight for freedom. The Bodyguards searching him before admission into the Bus, looked like street thugs. Broad shouldered, heavy handed street fighters with broken noses, certainly not the handsome Supermen pictured on campaign posters saying Governor Hominy wants your vote!

The Governor apologized for his bodyguards rough behavior. "You can't be too careful," he said. "There's a lot of Crazies out there gunning for me. I've made enemies who hate what I'm saying. Communists are everywhere, you know." He invited Dante to sit down and poured two glasses of Bourbon before continuing.

"Yes Sergeant I always knew something was different about that boy. He was so damn polite not like the poor white trash wandering the country, hitch-hiking or riding the rails going nowhere with their lives. He was good company for my Cora. Got along fine sitting together back of the bus holding hands like they was sweet on each other. I liked that. Made my little girl happy. Today, so many kids have no purpose, no discipline, no ambition except living from day to day with no tomorrow to look forward to. That's why my Youth Corps is so important to the future of our great nation. Get those poor kids out of the slums, out of the cities, get them working out in the clean fresh air of our wildernesses building up our country instead of tearing it down like the Reds are doing. There's nothing like discipline and hard work to make a man out of a boy! I Have no idea where he's gone to. He wasn't a shiftless no account like the jobless homeless Hoboes you see who don't want nothing better out of life. I always say you gotta make people want something different, give them hope, help them change their lives and it will happen! Prosperity will be just around the corner, a chicken will be in every pot, once I'm elected. And if you find that boy tell him for me he always welcome on my campaign bus. You know. Mi Casa. Su Casa."

Berl drained the last mouthful of water from his canteen hours ago. His parched throat seemed filled with sand. Feeling light-headed he rested on the roadside under the upraised arms of a Joshua tree that offered little protection from the heat. Exhausted, he closed his eyes to shut out the cruel glare of the mid-day sun dreaming he was looking out over the shimmering surface of a mountain lake. Cool clear water that saved his life. The raucous sound of an auto horn woke him from his reverie. Reluctantly he opened his eyes and saw the car's driver looking down at him shaking his head.

"I thought you was dead," the worried driver said. "Another damn fool trying to cross Death Valley with no hat, no water, and it's a hundred ten degrees in the shade, only there ain't none for fifty miles." He handed Berl a small canvas water bag. "Help yourself," he said. "This highway's lined with the bones of the ignorant who think they can make it without enough water." The driver led Berl into the backseat of his car occupied by two young women who were asleep.

"Be careful. Don't wake the girls," he said. "Sporting Girls can't take the heat no better than you, and I tell you good ones have been hard to find now crossing a state line with them is a felony." The driver paused and laughed defiantly. "Hell! a man's

The Prodigy

got to make a living no matter what the federal government says. And that's the God awful truth!"

"Sporting Girls?' Berl asked, confused.

"You don't know about Sporting Girls?" the driver replied. "No. Never heard of them," Berl explained, "I can see you ain't smart. Seems to me Roller skating is a damn fool way of travelling. Why when I was your age I'd seen most everything worth seeing and knew just about everything worth knowing like where I'm going on the road of life."

"Where is that?" Berl asked.

"The Chicken Ranch," the driver replied. " Best little Sporting House west of the Mississippi."

"Sporting House?" Berl asked, curious about his destination. The driver paused a moment before replying. "A place for good clean fun and sweet talk and if you're lonely and want company there's some of the prettiest "Sporting Girls" you've ever seen ready willing and able to haul your ashes. A dollar a minute. Fifteen dollars for fifteen minutes and if you don't have cash you can always bring a Chicken. That's why it's called the Chicken Ranch."

"I have fifteen dollars," Berl said. The driver shook his head. "Won't do you no good. Big Momma's strict about admitting juveniles. Except for college students come for initiations. What they call a "Rite of Passage". I tell you Big Momma's highly respected. Takes good care of her girls. Sees they stays sober and healthy living together like they was just one big family. Why some of the best wives in Nevada once worked at the Chicken Ranch."

Seated between the girls sleeping on the backseat of the car, Berl leaned back and recalled happy hours riding the campaign bus holding Cora in his arms, her head pillowed on his shoulder.

He remembered his first moments falling in love. Regretfully now only a painful memory. Travelling at night to evade the cruel desert heat, dehydrated by a long day in the sun, Berl fell asleep dreaming happy dreams of lying on his mother's warm breast as she sang a soothing lullaby. Then a voice gently said "My sweet little baby. Oh my sweet little baby." Two arms embraced him, pressing him against soft, perfumed flesh. Awakening, he did not move, fearing to lose the gift of such joy. "Oh my sweet little baby" the voice said again. "You make me so happy. You make me so happy." Berl awoke and looked up at a "Sporting Girl" who smiled as she leaned down and kissed him. A long passionate kiss. His loins erupted in a spasm of ecstasy. His heart stopped. His mind exploded at his first taste of the truly miraculous.

> Give me your tired,
> Your poor, your huddled masses
> yearning to breathe free,
> the wretched refuse of teeming shores.
> Send these, the homeless, tempest tossed to me,
> I lift my lamp beside the golden door.

Sergeant Emiliano Dante turned from his cluttered desk to look out his office window to watch the Ferries and Tug Boats navigating lower New York Bay. The Statue of Liberty, presiding over this scene evoked thoughts of what his father might have felt entering America's open door into the land of life, liberty and the pursuit of happiness.

Did his father shout? Cry out joyfully for this opportunity to make a new life in a land some immigrants called "The Golden Medina"? What did Giovanni feel discovering streets were not paved with gold and his destiny was to pave them with the sweat and tears of a hard life? Sergeant Dante turned away from the window and stared at his desk cluttered with Missing Person Dossiers. An endless parade of the lost, the dead, and the homeless. No need to stand on his head to know this world was turned upside down perhaps never to recover from a Depression sucking the vitality out of a great nation. Following leads evoked by generous rewards for information, Dante discovered there was a country, previously unknown to him, beyond the Hudson River. A land of foreclosed farms and homes, of bankrupt cities and abandoned factories, of long lines of the hungry waiting for a bowl of soup and a mouthful of bread. Of fathers and husbands struggling to retain their dignity and pride as bread winners. It was a land of voices crying out in a wilderness of despair hearing only other strident voices of hatred, fear and terror shouted by demagogues touring the country accompanied by motorcycle "Rough Riders" in leather jackets, and dark sunglasses.

How will all this end? Dante wondered. So many angry voices deepening a despair that leads only to violence. Voices proclaiming: "It is a terrible thing to kill. But we will kill not only others. We will kill ourselves too. For this murdering world can only be changed by force."

Dante recalled how in 1932 General Douglas MacArthur, head high, back straight, looking like a Roman Consul defended America against insurrection. From every state in the country seventeen thousand veterans, accompanied by wives and children, walked, drove or hitchhiked to Washington demanding their promised war bonuses from a reluctant Congress. Their tents and shacks encampment, called "Hooverville" to mock the feckless President, covered the Anacostia Flats riverbank across from the Capitol. Convinced he was opposing an attempt to overthrow the Government, General Macarthur ordered his masked soldiers to charge through clouds of tear gas into the camp with fixed bayonets, six tanks and mounted cavalry. Shots were fired. One thousand were injured. Four were dead. The wooden shacks and canvas tents were burned. The entire site and the veteran's belongings brutally destroyed. Bystanders witnessing "the Battle of Anacostia Flats" through rising clouds of black smoke cried: "Shame! Shame! Shame!"

But there was no shame in the Congress. Or a bonus quickly paid, Sergeant Dante remembered, thinking a nation's destructive power comes from not seeing its own evil. With self- righteousness killing conscience hatred and cruelty have taken the place of understanding. It's easier to fight than reconcile ambitions or dispel fears. Then, suddenly wondering about the motive for Berl's disappearance Sergeant Dante observed: there comes a time when a man must bet on himself even if it means staking his life on the outcome. There is one moment on which his whole life turns, requiring all his courage, and if he backs down from that challenge he is worthless.

SEVEN

California! The Promised Land! Tall palm trees swaying in the evening breeze! High Snow-capped mountains rising from deserts bordered by wild ocean beaches. Orange groves and fertile valleys as far as the eye can see. Berl skated across the State line singing "California Here I Come!" enjoying his moment of triumph. He made it! He arrived! With only the Pacific Ocean ending his westward journey to the land of dreamers, Emigrant survivors, religious Revivalists and aspiring movie stars. What next? he wondered. Where does he go now? What new destination, what new possibility can he look forward to? Quo Vadis? Where are you going was a question he could not answer.

Skating coastal highway 101, passing through small towns and larger villages, Berl was greeted by painted signs and flashing neon lights inviting travelers to stop and pray at many different roadside churches, tents and campgrounds where the faithful pursued and praised their personal Gods. A contagion of religious faith seemed to be in the air Californians breathed.

When Samuel Hope MD, otherwise known as "Smiling Sam" arrived at Berl's campground driving a truck loaded with wooden poles and rolls of canvas, he hired itinerant workmen to raise the tent in which he lectured and sold a book titled: *Take Command Of Your Life*. Berl, who had never held anything in his hands heavier than a violin case, when handed a hammer and a bundle of stakes lied about his ability to use them. A dollar a day after all is a dollar a day and high wages during the Depression were rare. Berl looked forward to earning money by physical labor. He helped raise the poles and erect a large canvas tent securing the ropes leading down from the pole tops to the stakes driven into the ground by sledge hammers. Berl raised his hammer high overhead and with all his strength swung down on the stakes. Again and again he struck hard. His arms and shoulders inflamed with pain. His eyes blinded by sweat. He continued pounding, driving the stakes deeper and deeper into the ground wondering was he injuring his hands? Destroying the sensitivity of fingers disciplined by years of practice?

Above the entrance to the tent a large portrait of Dr. Hope proclaimed: LIVE! LOVE! LAUGH AND BE HAPPY!

Attracted by this seductive call, the tent filled with life's walking wounded; the sick, the lame and the despairing yearning to be free of the pain of their daily lives. Berl walked through the crowd to the podium where the good Dr. Hope smiled and laughed and waving his arms welcomed the hopeful. Rising from wheelchairs, throwing aside crutches, chanting "Love and a hug! Love and a hug!" the audience danced around the podium, legs pounding the ground, arms reaching out to hold each other in an ecstatic frenzy that excited Berl. "Live! Love! Laugh and be Happy" the doctor sang again and again. "Live! Love! Laugh and be Happy!" The dancers responded shouting "Love and a Hug! Love and a Hug!" in one overpowering voice that made the tent walls tremble. Berl opened his arms as if to embrace the dancers, head high, back straight, he began dancing, merging with the crowd celebrating life's joy. Berl danced toward the light radiating from Dr. Hope. A compelling force he never felt before embraced him, evoking a feeling of oneness with a power he could not name. He no longer felt like an isolated creature obsessed by his determination to live and travel the world apart from the family of Man. His true family. He turned and smiled at the audience's shining faces dancing beside him and saw the love that unites mankind. For the first time in his life he felt the glory of faith. Faith in a guiding power in the Universe. Faith in something larger than himself. Faith that keeps the world sane. Faith in a mystery that makes living possible. Banish that mystery and you have nothing but death. Yes. There is a land of the living, Berl recognized, and a land of the dead, and the bridge between them is love for only love survives. And if God is love, then he most certainly believed in God! Berl began to tremble as he accepted his place in the Universe. Yes! He belonged here on this good earth, he was a part of this world of sun and sky and fertile farmlands reaching out to beckoning horizons and never again would he fear being alone, a solitary prisoner of fate. He was now liberated. In command of his life.

Yes, said Sergeant Dante thinking about his Uncle who never immigrated to America, there's a lot of Evil in this world. Like the Evil done by Italian Fascisti led by Dictator Benito Mussolini using political violence to win elections.

The Prodigy

Remembering his father reading his brother's final letter sobbing "He was killed for shouting "A basso Mussolini! Viva Liberta!" Dante asked himself, -- can this happen here? Innocent men tortured to death? Lives sacrificed fighting for freedom? Could this ever happen in the good old USA?

Reading headlines about Henry Ford rejecting Collective Bargaining, deny his workers' rights, Dante was outraged. Frightened by fifty Union Organizers distributing pamphlets and circulars informing employees of their rights, Ford hired mobsters to fight the "Battle of the Overpass" at his Michigan River Rouge plant. Fracturing skulls, breaking backs, smashing faces into the ground they defied the rule of Law. Henry Ford believed he was defending Law and Order. Government officials called out the National Guard, brought in the army and declared Martial Law to break strikes with bayonets and gunfire that left a dozen dead and dozens wounded. Prohibiting mass meetings, hundreds of demonstrators were jailed and released only after they signed anti-union pledges. In Homestead Pennsylvania, Pinkerton Agents fought day-long gun battles and during the "Red Scare", War Veterans and Tradesmen were deputized to break Communist inspired strikes. Yes indeed Labor's search for more paid a high price in blood and terror. What Sergeant Dante once believed impossible, seemed now possible. Motorcycle "Rough Riders" with sirens drowning out protesting voices, knocked down and dispersed demonstrators opposing "Bull" Hominy. Breaking legs, smashing speaker's platforms, Governor Hominy's Storm Troopers fulfilled his pledge to maintain order convinced civil disobedience is anarchy and only "Bull" Hominy can keep the Barbarians outside the wall protecting law-abiding citizens. Sergeant Dante's now had the answer to his question -- Yes! it can happen here.

In Los Angeles, also known as La La land, Berl skated down Sunset Boulevard passing the palatial mansions of Hollywood's famous movie stars. Tall Palm trees swaying in Pacific ocean breezes lined the avenue leading Berl into a world of make-believe. The air perfumed by orange blossoms, uncontaminated by smog, created a feeling of seductive freedom in an extraordinary city, a fascinating Paradise populated by hopeful performers pursuing dreams of future stardom competing for attention in bizarre costumes and startling make up. Cowboys and Indians, African Witch Doctors and half-dressed Tarzans shared sidewalks and parks with full-breasted ingénues bursting out of tight sweaters. Studio Back-lots recreated replicas of foreign Castles and Cathedrals, Western Cow towns and Main Street America in astonishing detail. At night bright searchlights illuminated the sky celebrating another fabulous movie premier. Wherever Berl looked he saw wealth and glamour, an exotic culture that believed nothing succeeds like excess.

Several miles away skating to Los Angeles' Griffith Park, Berl saw an encampment of destitute victims of the Great Depression. Sheltered in tents and wooden shacks, surviving on a bowl of soup a day, despised as homeless Drifters, the hungry and unemployed living in the park asked that heart-breaking question -- "Buddy can you spare a dime?" In a year of remarkable adventures Berl had not encountered a more disturbing scene. Shocked and breathless, he sat down on a park bench to think about this contrast between poverty and great wealth that defied his understanding. How was this possible? How could this have happened in such a beautiful country?

As if responding to his query, an old man on a nearby bench turned and asked: "What in God's name have you got on your feet?"

"Roller skates," Berl replied. "Nothing but Roller skates." The old man nodded. "Don't think I ever seen them before. Looks like fun."

"It can be," Berl replied. "When it's not raining."

"Well, you come to the right state. Not much rain in California." Wearing a French Beret lowered over one eye, equestrian's jodhpurs and polished riding boots, the old man raised his cane and with the gracious dignity of genteel poverty pointed at the crowded park. "Now that park's as real as any crowd scene in one of my movies" the old man said, shaking his head, smiling as he recalled a happy memory. "I always directed Budget-busters," he said, "Four hundred Extras. Two hundred tents. And fifty wooden shacks for the police to burn down."

"What's an Extra?" Berl asked. Trying to understand. The old man lowered the cane to the ground before replying.

"Extras are just bodies who fill out a scene. For a few dollars a day they make it look real."

"Like in the park?" Berl asked. "That's right," the old man replied, laughing. "A movie scene must always look real even though it's make believe. Producers always screamed bankruptcy when I showed them my scripts. I knew what I wanted. Lots of Extras. Always got my way. Never lost a fight with those penny-pinching Assholes. There was never anything small about what I directed. Never directed low budge crap. Shit between sprocket holes." Emotionally drained, the old man paused to catch his breath.

"Now Buster Keaton, Harold Lloyd, Charlie Chaplin, Doug Fairbanks, Hal Roach and Cecil B. De Mille were great directors. Had big dreams of what a movie should be. They invented this business."

"What are you directing now?" Berl asked.

The Old man shook his head. "Haven't worked in five years. Couldn't stand those God damn microphones and high-brow scripts. Movies are nothing but pictures and action and once they began talking there's no more silent films. Directors are now nothing but traffic cops photographing pages of dialogue." The old man turned and looked at Berl. "Tell me young man, who is your favorite movie star?"

"I don't have one," Berl replied.

The old man stared at Berl. Incredulous. "Don't you ever go to the movies?" he asked. "No." Berl said. "That's hard to believe," the old man replied shaking his head. "You never heard of Shirley Temple?"

"Who is she?" Berl asked.

"Why she's a little girl who captured the heart of America! She could dance, sing and make audiences laugh and cry. Gets more fan mail than

America's sweetheart, Lillian Gish." The old man tapped his cane on the ground as if demanding attention to what he is about to say. "Anyone who never been to a movie or doesn't know about Shirley Temple and Lillian Gish is Un-American! Why movies are America! Who we are! Land of the Free! Home of the Brave! You can see our whole country up there on the silver screen. America the beautiful. Why movies are more powerful than the Government with FDR not knowing how to get us out of the Depression Walt Disney turned the country around with his Mickey Mouse and Who's afraid of the Big Bad Wolf! Saved us from a revolution."

"How did they do that?" Berl asked.

The old man paused recalling the past. "They did away with fear," he said. "Paralyzing fear. People didn't know what to do. What was coming next. Going to the movies they could forget their troubles. Learn they had nothing to fear but fear itself."

"Yes, Sergeant Dante, when the President called me the most dangerous man in America -- he was right! I'm against everything that cripple, that anti-Christ in the White House believes. He's ruining our beloved country, destroying our freedom with Satan inspired deceptions. He's for corruption, depravity, and decadence and I'll fight him until the End of Time. I have my rendezvous with Destiny keeping America free and safe for Americans. Only an assassins' bullet can stop me. That's why I have Bodyguards and bullet proof glass windows on my Bus. I have enemies. Jews! Communists! Bankers!

And all the other un-Godly Atheists destroying our good old USA. And you know, one bullet can change everything! One bullet can start a war. Change the world and kill 10 million people. It's not I am afraid of dying but not until I've done what God asked me to do. Yes siree! Save my people. Work for the Little Man who never can make something out of his life. Have his own home, raise a family, have a good job! Now you tell me – is this too much to ask? Too much to expect from a government of the people. By the people and for the people. Like Lincoln I'm going to bind up our nation's wounds. Comfort the poor and make the rich uncomfortable. Some people hate me. You wouldn't believe how many letters I get accusing me of wanting to overthrow our government and be a Dictator when all I want is to right what's wrong. And what's so wrong with that? That's what Jesus tried to do. And Moses leading his people to the Promised land. Nothing good ever happens without a strong leader. Someone with a vision of what the future can be. Someone determined to fight for what's right even though he gets killed trying. So you see Sergeant Dante, I've come a long way from where I started. Been dirt poor. Hungry. Seen people I love sick and dying before their time. Seen what it's like to live without hope. Without a chance to get something out of life. That's why I still have a long way to go, Sergeant Dante, a long way to go after I get into the White House."

Hollywood Studios were fabulous factories producing adventure, romance and fantasy films to provide an escape from the Great Depression.

The Prodigy

Telling stories in Re-created Villages and Kingdoms, snow capped mountains, exotic deserts and placid lakes, American movies entertained audiences around the world with exciting dramas that stirred the imagination. From the small towns, villages and cities of America aspiring performers came to Hollywood dreaming futile dreams of stardom. A few became only "bit" players speaking one line of dialogue. Most were silent "Extras". Every morning, outside Studio gates, long lines of the hungry and destitute waited impatiently hoping to earn five dollars a day in crowd scenes. Tall and short. Thin and fat. Old and young. Male and female, these anonymous bodies gave a feeling of reality to spectacular movies. Removing his roller skates, Berl waited in a long line of the hopeful and was soon hired. Dressed in a tattered, bloodstained soldier's uniform he was placed among other battlefield casualties depicting the horrors of war. Instructed to appear dead, and not to breathe or move, Berl refused saying: "If I stop breathing I will die."

"What are you a wise-guy?" The Director exploded.

"No sir," Berl replied. "I just want to live."

"What's your name," the Director asked. "Where you from?"

"New York. And my name is Berl."

"My God! Another wise-ass New Yorker!" The Director shouted.

"No sir," Berl said.

"If you move or breathe while the camera is rolling I personally will come and kill you!" the Director threatened angrily. "I wouldn't like that."

Berl answered, shaking his head. Stunned by the response.

"I will cut you up in little pieces and use you in the morgue scene."

"Maybe I better stay on the battlefield?" Berl said, promising "I'll try not to breathe."

"Or move!" the Director shouted again. "Not one muscle! Not one finger! Not one eyelash! You keep your stupid eyes closed until I shout Cut!"

"Yes sir," Berl replied.

"It's hard work making a scene look real," the Director explained.

"I should think so," Berl answered.

"One false move, one little mistake and you destroy the illusion of reality."

"Yes sir."

"In movies seeing is believing and what you see is what you're going to get," the Director insisted. "That's why it's important you look dead even though you're alive. You understand?"

"Yes sir," Berl said, nodding agreement. "I understand." The Director turned and walked away from Berl. Stopping suddenly, as if struck by a brilliant thought, he raised a hand-held view finder to his eye and began framing Berl from several angles. "My God! My God! He shouted. "You're just what I'm looking for!"

Berl, playing dead, remained motionless on the battlefield. Holding his breath. "Stand up!" the Director ordered. "Stand up so I can get a good look at you!"

"You mean I'm not dead anymore?" Berl asked.

"Just stand up!" the Director insisted as he studied Berl. "You're the right height. Turn and show me your profile." Berl rising and brushing dirt from his blood-stained uniform asked. "Can I breathe now?" The Director put down the view-finder and embraced Berl. "How would you like a promotion?" he asked. "A raise in pay. No more drowning in the mud covered with blood?"

"I'd like that," Berl replied.

"You ever hear of Bobby Benson?" the Director asked.

"No."

"He's a big Star. Very popular. We're producing a series of pictures with him playing a healthy All American Boy in an ideal family. You're his size. Not too tall. Not too short."

"His size?" Berl asked.

"For being his Stand In," the Director explained.

"What's a Stand In?"

"Every Star got one. Someone to stand in front of the camera while the hot lights are adjusted keeps the Star from being tired and sweating."

"I never sweat," Berl said. Fascinated by the careful labor of setting-up a shot Berl walked, turned and remained motionless as the Klieg lights were adjusted, the dolly tracks laid, and the camera movements rehearsed. A compliant Stand-in, he followed directions without question or pause impressed by the quiet efficiency of a movie crew. Electricians, soundmen, make-up artists, and hard-working Grips worked as a team under the impatient guidance of the Director struggling to complete three pages of script a day. Some described making movies as organized chaos with a shouting cost-conscious Producer urging everyone to keep moving on to the next set-up.

Bobby Benson, the "All American Boy," abused all the obnoxious prerogatives of a popular movie Star. Appearing late on the set, forgetting his lines, arguing with the Director, he often failed to hit his marks under the Key light or speak within range of the microphones. He sometimes required three walks through a door before successfully coordinating with the camera. Re-enforcing his self-confidence with Vodka, his blurred speech made his performances unprintable even after six or more "Takes." He was a disaster waiting to happen. Tolerated because of the Fan Mail testifying to his popularity. He was a "Bankable Star" essential to financing a production. At Box Offices in theaters throughout America Bobby Benson was pure gold.

Sticks and stone can break your bones – but Hate Mail can kill! Sergeant Dante reminded himself as he watched the evening TV news showing Governor "Bull" Hominy wading through crowds of wildly cheering spectators. Reaching out to embrace admirers, shaking hands, kissing babies, the Governor repeated this ritual several times a day in a remarkable demonstration of fearless political determination. Assassination can happen to any candidate, Sergeant Dante thought recalling the attack on FDR that killed the Mayor of Miami. It's all a matter of luck, good or bad Dante concluded thinking of the virulent power of fear and hatred. The fuel that powers the engine of Politics. Hominy's Bodyguards were well-trained shielding him within a moving protective formation of Rough Riders scanning spectators for any sign of danger, pledged to stop a bullet with their bodies.

The Prodigy

Sergeant Dante sang: -- my country tis of thee sweet land of bigotry of thee I sing. Yes indeed! assassination is as American as apple pie. Violence is the language we speak. That's how we create history. Lincoln, Garfield, McKinley, Teddy Roosevelt, Mayor Cermak, FDR and Huey Long. All seven assassinated, and eight is not a lucky number. With fear mongers in the press and on radio frightening mindless voters, Governor "Bull" Hominy will need more than four bodyguards to survive his enemies' irrational fury Sergeant Dante concluded.

"The business of America is business," said President Calvin Coolidge during the roaring twenties when a "Hit Man" charged a hundred dollars to eliminate a business rival or an unwanted spouse. In Chicago, Dutch Schultz and Al Capone, fought their Gangland Wars disputing territories they could shake down in the dark underbelly of America. Mobs massacred each other in what the tabloid press called the great American "Crime Wave". *Scarface* with Paul Muni was the year's most popular movie. Quo Vadis? Where are we going? Sergeant Dante wondered. What is happening in an America where J. Edgar Hoover's "G Men" are celebrated for killing John Dillinger, Bonny and Clyde, and Baby Face Nelson in "The War on Crime". Maybe for America Law and order is an impossible dream?

Spectacular in its beauty and danger, California's "Big Sur section of the Pacific Coast Highway was a narrow two lane road cut into cliffs descending to wild ocean beaches. A hazardous

110

winding road without a safety barrier separated a car from a thousand foot drop to the rocks below where turbulent surf batters and carries out to sea the wreckage of both man and machine. Some call this "the Highway of Death". Others consider it a trip through Paradise with magnificent vistas as far as the eye can see.

Bobby Benson had no appreciation of scenic beauty and grandeur. His great passion was speed. Driving his imported Lancia Grand Prix racing car he felt the power of a young God in control of fate. With only a few inches separating his wheels from the edge of precipice he played a dangerous game and lost. Neither his body or car wreckage were ever recovered. Only a metal cross and a small bronze plaque on the roadside memorialized the passing of the All American Boy.

With five more days needed to complete Bobby Benson's last film, Berl became his "Double". Subdued lighting kept his face in shadows and photographing over his shoulder, side or rear enabled Berl to successfully replace the Star whose death no one mourned. Berl was a pleasure to work with. A real Professional. His years concertizing taught him to always arrive on time and never question the Director.

It was generally agreed that Pappa Pincus was a beautiful human being. Owner, founder and the Boss of Colossal Pictures, Hollywood's oldest and largest studio, he was a "Mogul with a heart". Colossal Pictures was one big family with Pappa dispensing paternal guidance to his always troubled "stable" of movie stars. To be under contract to Colossal was to have a home away from home. Alcoholism, infidelity and divorces were bad for the studio's image of producing wholesome family oriented entertainment and displeasing Pappa Pincus ended many promising careers. Without children of his own, the warmest spot in Pappa big heart was his devotion to the well being and education of his surrogate family of adolescent movie stars. The studio's High school exceeded the standards of California's child labor and education laws and successfully dismissed accusations he was exploiting child actors. He reminded Berl of the Impresario Ziggy Goldfarb who showed him the love and affection withheld by his parents.

It was love at first sight. In Pappa's eyes Berl was a better "All American Boy", the studio's most popular role to be performed by Berl as the new Bobby Benson. Roller skating from the Atlantic to the Pacific hardened Berl's body from adolescence to young manhood. He was taller, the Child Prodigy now a young Adventurer prepared to meet any challenge. And Pappa's demands were more than a challenge. They were inviolable commandments. A sentimental vision of what the American family should be with an adored mother, a wise forgiving father and a respectful son. Bobby Benson didn't smoke or drink and had a chaste relationship with his girlfriend. When confronted by teen-age troubles he sat down for a father and son discussion where wisdom and understanding brought forth heart-breaking sobs as Bobby Benson recognized the error of his transgressions. The hearts and minds of America welcomed this idealized vision of the family with a loving mother generously dispensing hugs and kisses as the music swelled to a tear-jerking crescendo at the final Fade Out.

How the money rolled in! A tidal wave of fan letters overwhelmed the mailroom. And Pappa Pincus now had a new son on whom he could ply his sly and profitable magic.

"An All American Boy," Pappa Pincus explained, "always does his best, and when he does something wrong corrects his faults guided by his father's wisdom. An All American Boy is honorable and trustworthy and when his dog is dying gets down on his knees and prays to God to save his beloved pet. The All American Boy in movie theaters across America teaches other boys how to live their lives. He adores his mother. Her every wish is his command and father is like a God. No matter what the wise guys say, I can make money producing movies without violence, without brutality, without Cowboys and Indians and the Cavalry riding to rescue the wagon train." He paused a moment to recover his composure before putting into words his Mantra, his mission in life. "I can produce movies that make our beloved country a better place in which to raise our children."

Papa Pincus paused a moment and then turned to study Berl before nodding thoughtfully and asking: "What was your family like?"

"Not like Bobby Bensons'," Berl replied. "You had a father and a mother?"

"Yes," Berl said. "But we didn't talk to each other like in your movies."

"Why is that? Pappa asked.

"I don't know," Berl replied.

"I want you to know," Pappa said with an inviting smile, "My office door is always open. Anytime you want to talk to me I'm here to listen. You might say I'm your Pappa now."

"I'd like that," Berl replied. "Thank you."

"I want you to know you have a great responsibility," Pappa continued. "Everything up there on the silver screen affects millions of lives for good or for bad. Everything you do is important which is why you must always obey the director. He knows what's best for you."

"Who will be my mother?" Berl asked.

"Well you might say I am both your father and your mother," Pappa Pincus replied. "Two parents are better than one."

The assassination was shown in every newsreel theater in America in a documentary program called "The March of Time!" Sergeant Dante watched the film several times thinking this was not the act of some crazed mental defective or "Lone Wolf" misfit. This killing was the planned precise shooting of three snipers. A coordinated triangulation. A military operation. Perhaps a possible coup? Motorcycle "Rough Riders" with sirens blaring and motors roaring, escorted the campaign Bus through a sea of spectators chanting "Every Man A King! -- Every Man A King!" The Governor stepped out of the door and waded through the crowd shaking outstretched hands, kissing babies, escorted by Bodyguards scanning faces for any possible threat. A precaution re-enacted several times a day during an election campaign. Suddenly three simultaneous gunshots followed by hysterical screams incited immediate panic. Spectators threw themselves on the ground or ducked for cover while Cora, the Governor's daughter held her dying father in her arms sobbing "No! No! No!"

The "Rough Riders" escorting the Governor blocked the Hospital entrance holding back the crowds of Journalists and newsreel cameras popping flashbulbs and illuminating the scene with flood lights. An emotional Inferno, thought Sergeant Dante, an uncontrolled mob. And on radio and in theaters across the country a Narrator's deep voice intoned an obituary: "Death, as it must come to all men, has come to Governor "Bull" Hominy. Feared by some as a potential dictator. Loved by others as their Savior, "Bull" Hominy lived the great American story. The dream of rising from poverty, from the choking dust of cotton fields to the Governor's chair in one of our nation's most vital states. He was best known for his enemies. The economic and political powers that for generations ruled his homeland. Governor "Bull" Hominy will never be forgotten by the poor, the homeless, the unemployed. He gave them more than the promise of jobs. He gave his followers hope and a vision of a life free of poverty and disease. Our nation has suffered a grievous loss."

Sergeant Dante walked out of the newsreel theater in despair convinced Hominy was a fraud. The nation would be safer without him.

Thinking about Miriam, Menahim's mother, Sergeant Dante understood her shoplifting spree when unhappy creditors closed her unpaid credit card accounts. Her insatiable appetite for expensive clothing, jewelry, shoes, hats, and lingerie could only be satisfied by theft. Dressed in a luxurious Mink coat and a designer hat, she wandered through Bloomingdales Department store her nimble fingers adorned with diamond rings reaching out to snatch whatever glittering bauble aroused her desire for more of everything. Sergeant Dante's most difficult "Person of Interest", after months listed as "address unknown" finally surfaced in a Police station holding Cell. No longer a "Submarine" concealed in the depths of a great City, Miriam was now available for questioning.

"Let me tell you Sergeant Dante I'm no thief. had every intention of paying. I simply forgot what was in my handbag when I walked out of the store. I have been called many horrible names but thief is certainly not one of them. I despise people who lie and cheat. I'm too honest for my own good like when asked why Menahim was not concertizing I told them the truth and was crucified by music critics who always hated me. They are blood sucking vultures feeding off the talent of serious performers breaking their hearts and spirit with destructive reviews. I ask you who gave them the right to be so cruel? To say who shall live and who shall die as artists? I have lived my whole life for Menahim and have no idea why he is doing what he is doing by refusing to play. I ask you how could he do this to me a mother who only did what was best for his career. Life's unfair. That such a talented boy should punish his mother for what he thinks she did. Something he finds unacceptable. Immoral. Unethical. So now he throws away his life and a brilliant career hiding out in Paradise Lodge like some sort of a God sitting in holy righteous judgment on a mother who never pretended to be a Saint. I did whatever was necessary for my boy to win. What any loving mother would do."

LIGHTS!... CAMERA!... ACTION!... three imperative commands shouted through a megaphone began the daily production of motion pictures in Hollywood's fabulous studios. More than two hundred new films a year met the world's insatiable need for entertainment. As Bobby Benson, "The All American Boy", Berl felt part of something larger than himself conveying Pappa Pincus' idealistic vision of a better world. That making movies also involved working with fools, liars and knaves didn't surprise Berl. He thought the writers, directors and producers guiding his career lived superficial lives devoid of deep feeling. "Tinsel Town" seemed a lost city ruled by a boy wonder called "The Vine Street Jesus" who casually made and destroyed careers motivating disappointed castoffs to end their dreams of stardom by diving off Pasadena's notorious "Suicide Bridge." Now a popular, money-making Star popularized by Hedda Hopper and Louella Parsons in "Variety", Hollywood's New Testament, Berl's celebrated life alternated between holiday and farce and sometimes tragedy. He felt he lived and worked in a mongrel world speeding towards some fatal destiny no one could evade. He was the epicenter of a whirlpool of cameras, lights, microphones, and the fan mail of screaming admirers wherever he travelled. He had become the end product of a fast moving assembly line of skilled craftsmen planning, writing and rewriting, casting, constructing, lighting, rehearsing, shooting and editing movies that were like the magical substance Manna given to Israelites wandering the Sinai desert. Staring at his roller skates mounted on his dressing room wall, Berl recalled the freedom he had surrendered and lost, the joy of knowing that tomorrow would bring something new. As Bobby Benson he was a prisoner of demanding directors and producers and distributors concerned only with budgets and production schedules. Yes! He had come a long way from Carnegie Hall only to arrive at the quandary he tried to escape from. Yes! It is true, Berl discovered, the more the soul grows old, the harder it is to escape one's fate.

Joan La Motte had a heart as big as a hotel where there was always room for young aspiring movie actors in her luxurious Bridal Suite. After her years of fabulous stardom were eclipsed by the addition of sound to movies, Joan La Motte's glamour never faded. Tall, curvaceous, with an enigmatic face that delighted cameramen, she had an exotic look of sexual temptation combined with child-like innocence that delighted silent film audiences. Her career crashed when she spoke. Her rumbling whiskey voice shattered her appearance of walking in beauty both day and night. Her retirement was devoted to seducing the innocent and handsome who like Berl were attracted to her web of lies and illusion. And what Joan La Motte wants she always gets with charm and guile and perseverance.

Berl was a new boy in town unacquainted with Hollywood's social quicksand determined by power and position. Joan La Motte became his mentor showing him who was, and who was not worth knowing. Who could and who could not advance his career for inevitably he would soon outgrow the role of the "All American Boy."

"Learn how to play the Hollywood game," Joan La Motte advised Berl, "you're in a Gambling Casino where losers far outnumber the winners. Learn the tricks of the trade and you will have a brilliant future."

"The tricks of the trade?" asked Berl. "

Yes. An ounce of illusion is worth more than a pound of reality. It isn't who you are and what you can do, it's who you know. No contract is worth more than the paper it is written on. And beware of pity. Don't feel sorry for the losers, fallen stars are as numerous as those in the sky. And never get on the bad side of our twenty-five year old boy wonder, the production genius running the studio. He will drive you out of town if you don't kiss his ass."

"Is that what happened to you? Berl asked.

"Hell no! I would have slept with him to save my career only he never asked. He preferred his playmates young and nubile"

When Sergeant Emiliano Dante heard the bad news on the radio he immediately drove to Paradise Lodge to complete his Menahim Dossier. With the Sanitarium's therapeutic tranquility shattered by reporters and newsreel cameras crowding the driveway, Dr. Franz Frankel, famous for reviving celebrities who are in despair, refused to answer shouted questions of unhappy journalists searching for a lurid page one story.

"Patient confidentiality prohibits answering your questions," Dr. Frankel insisted. "You must wait for the Coroner's report."

The raucous uproar continued: "I can assure you there is no cover-up," Dr. Frankel said. "No question of medical malfeasance." He then entered the building closing the doors as the reporters turned away shouting their disappointment.

Waiting in Dr. Frankel's office, Sergeant Dante held up a document saying: "I have a Court Order. Menahim was a Person of Interest in an open investigation. You must answer a few questions." Doctor Frankel nodded. Fighting back tears.

"There was not much we could do to save the boy," Dr. Frankel said. "Not after his mother reappeared after six months without a phone call or a letter. Totally uninterested in her son's recovery. Some animals eat their young you know. Kill them when they are unwanted or of no further use. Mommy dearest was a woman without a heart or a conscience. A murderer. I don't know what she told her son but whatever she said was catastrophic. That's when Menahim began sliding down the slippery slope to a deep and intractable depression. I put him on a twenty-four hour suicide watch only he was too far gone to even be capable of another overdose attempt. Electro-shock is always the therapy of last resort. It's an admission of failure when all our other efforts do not prevail. And I hate failure. Find it totally unacceptable. Bad for my reputation. Everyone here at Paradise Lodge loved him. He was kind and gentle unprepared for the world's cruelty and his mother's brutality. We didn't know he had an undiagnosed heart condition. His EKG was perfectly normal."

In Hollywood, nothing succeeds like excess! Joan La Motte's Boudoir, her Promised Land, was more carefully designed than any glamorous movie set serving as background for scenes of passionate love. Soft music, exotic flowers, candlelight, and perfumed air provided the ambience for a thousand and one nights of unbridled lust. In the center of this web, Joan La Motte's alluring body in a transparent negligee invited handsome young men to explore their sexuality. After a long hard day as Bobby Benson the "All American Boy," Berl welcomed her invitation to a mid-night supper where he had an opportunity to perform the more difficult role of a Lover. No longer an adolescent, his previous unconsummated affairs unhappy memories, Berl's fear of failure, of looking ridiculous, aroused in him the humiliating anxiety of a virgin. Greeted at the door of her Beverly Hills Mansion by a Japanese Butler who was also her chauffer and bodyguard, Berl followed him up a long stairway to the gateway to Paradise where a smiling Joan La Motte, holding a long fashionable cigarette holder in one hand, opened her welcoming arms and gave him a quick greeting kiss on each cheek.

"My dear Boy," she said, taking his hand and leading him into her bedroom. Berl followed entering a large candle lit chamber with thick golden drapes covering the windows. The low table in front of a sofa held Champagne, glasses, and a bucket of Caviar. "You must be thirsty," she continued, "I know what it is like to work those long brutal hours under those cruel hot lights." She poured two glasses of champagne offering one to Berl. "If wine makes a woman glamorous and Champagne makes a woman amorous," she said, asking her favorite riddle, "What makes a woman hot?" Raising the glass to his lips Berl hesitated thoughtfully before admitting: "I don't know. You tell me. What makes a woman hot?" Joan La Motte paused for a long moment smiling as she replied in her rasping voice: "Two highballs and a straight!" Berl laughed politely as his hostess acknowledged his response with an endearing smile. "I like a good joke," she said. "Life has become so grim these days. What with the Depression and all this talk of war it's no wonder everyone is so depressed. And the movies they're producing I find unbearable. Nothing but rape and murder and dead bodies wherever you look corrupting our country with their insidious stories. Did you know the movie screen is the entrance to the very soul of America?" Berl shook his head. "I didn't know that," he replied. "How about Bobby Benson?" he asked. Joan La Motte laughed, drained and then refilled her glass. "Candy for children. Make believe like the Sunday comics," she said dismissively. "Movies should fill our souls with beauty and a sense of wonder about the miracle of life! Movies should help us understand and cope with this terrifying world in which we live. My movies were an affirmation and not a degradation of mankind. My movies were an artistic cry for help in a trivial, indifferent and easily entertained world that has lost all sympathetic feelings for each other." Joan La Motte again refilled her glass. "Did you ever see me do the dance of the Seven Veils in

Salome she asked. "No," Berl replied. "I haven't seen many movies." Joan La Motte put down her glass and rose from the couch. "Now this is what I call great Art. Salome belly dancing in front of King Herod who seduced, presents her with John the Baptist' head on a silver tray. That dance was the greatest scene in my fabulous career." Joan La Motte turned on a record player filling the room with the wild sounds of a flute and a drum and cymbals, and opening her flowing robes, reached out her arms as if to embrace all the lovers in the world as her sinuous body danced across the room, her hips and belly rotating around the middle of a moving center of love and lust. Berl watched from the couch enthralled. Aroused. And when Salome danced in front of him, her seductive belly and hips thrusting towards him in lascivious joy, Berl fled from the room.

Bobby Benson's co-star, Bunny Bingham, the "All American Girl" who adored her father, loved her mother, feared God and was chaste with her boyfriends, was also vain, thoughtless and self absorbed. "Look but don't touch my body" was the Cardinal rule of the romantic game she played with Berl on and off the movie set. Attracting and rejecting, smiling and frowning, friendly and distant, she stoked the burning embers of Berl's desire. He fell in love with an adolescent vixen with no hope of consummation. Marriage was not in the script. Indeed, Bunny Bingham's entire life was an unfinished movie written by an ambitious mother who drove a five year old child to future stardom with dancing, singing and acting lessons that became the only life Bunny knew. At the end of each day, when the cameras stopped rolling and the hot lights were turned off, Bunny Bingham felt a depressing sadness as she came down from the exhilarating highs of the roles she played where happiness was endless and Life was a Ball. Everything beyond the Studio's walls was dull and unsatisfying. Not dancing, singing or acting was a little death. A fear she could never subdue. And so each morning at dawn, as the makeup artists and hairdressers prepared her for the day's performance in front of the cameras, Bunny Bingham felt herself come truly alive for one more day as the "All American Girl."

Berl didn't know the language unlocking a woman's heart. His kind sweet words didn't win Bunny and soon he concluded that if by himself if he could not make her, then let the Devil take her. He would wait for the deep feelings possessing his soul, the pain of rejection, vanish with time. And anyway, what is love? What did he really feel for Cinderella? For Cora? For Bunny? Maybe love is more trouble than it's worth? His love of his parents yielded only pain and exploitation. Only the Impresario Ziggy Goldfarb and Menahim never disappointed him. Were worthy of his love. His enduring love. And so every day in front of the cameras he pretended to enjoy the vivacious company of his movie girl friend who, when the director shouted "Cut and Print," reverted to being a destructive Bitch.

Bunny Bingham's predatory future as a heart breaker included six failed marriages, alcoholism, drug addiction, three face-lifts and annual Rehab visits to fashionable Clinics known for their famous Clientele. At her spectacular funeral three thousand adoring fans crowded the entrance to the church to watch the parade of celebrity mourners consisting of several co-stars, two millionaire business executives, one Congressman, and an alcoholic Poet. Her Eulogy described all the good she had done with her life and career. The Charities, the Homeless Shelters, the Food Banks, the Baby Clinics for unwed mothers made possible by her generosity. Certainly Bunny Bingham's life exemplifies what one person can do to make the world a better place to live.

Berl was very much alive performing in front of the camera, signing autographs for adoring fans, making personal appearances and working with the Studio Publicity department. An exhausting life requiring drugs for a good night's sleep. When he learned of Menahim's death his rising star shattered and fell to earth. Secluded in his darkened bedroom he closed the curtains attempting to shut out the reality of his sorrow and the pain of his regret. His dear friend, his love was no more, destroyed by the embarrassment of an award he did not believe he deserved. And so Berl learned life was cruel and unfair and love treacherous and he vowed to never again be trapped in its quicksand. Love, he believed, inevitably resulted in unbearable loss and the inability to think and feel and somehow find the resilience to endure a broken-heart. When after several weeks he returned to work the adolescent innocence of the "All American Boy" was gone. He walked through performances, followed direction without enthusiasm unable to project the happiness his fans expected. Box office receipts declined. Critics now considered Berl too old to be a role model for the youth of America. Pappa Pincus was worried.

"You must get over it, Pappa advised sympathetically. "All of life involves loss. That's what life is all about. Live long enough and everything good and bad will happen to you. You must learn what can not be cured must be endured."

Berl remained silent. Refusing to be consoled.

"Think of all the good you have done," Papa said. "Think of the millions of fans you have inspired to live healthier, happier lives. Think of all the parents who thank you for helping them show their children how to live a better life." Papa paused for a moment reaching out to take Berl's hand. "And remember you have a responsibility to all who have made you rich and famous."

"I don't believe in the All American Boy any more," Berl said quietly. "I want to grow up. For ten years I've been playing Bobby Benson. I want to be an adult."

"I understand," Papa replied. "No one wants to remain a boy forever." Papa put his arm about Berl. Hugging him. "I have big plans for you when you finish this production. A real grown up role."

"Like what?" Berl asked.

"Like Paganini," Papa said enthusiastically. "Paganini! The inspiration of my life. For twenty years I've dreamed of making a movie about Paganini, the greatest violin virtuoso of all times. One of the greatest stories that's never been filmed."

"Why not?" Berl asked.

"Why not?" Papa replied. "Why not? I'll tell you why not! This town's filled with actors who are nothing more than pretty boys. Stars for women to dream about. Worth their weight in gold at the Box office but without the sensitivity, the beauty of a great artistic soul they could never play the part. Bring Paganini back to life on every movie screen in America." Papa hesitated, describing his great dream. "Think about his life," Papa said. "A Boy genius. A violin virtuoso from the age of five. Travelling with his father to all the great cities of Europe. Adored by Royalty. Concertizing in the world's greatest theaters and Opera Houses. A rising Star overwhelming audiences with the magnificence of his artistry. Critics declared only someone who made a pact with the Devil could have such musical power. Then from the pinnacle of his career his fall. His tragic decline. Drinking. Gambling. Womanizing. Tuberculosis. Financial ruin. Abandoned by friends and the women he ruined he dies alone with the Church denying him a Christian burial believing his playing was the work of the Devil." Papa nodded and waved his finger at Berl. "You could be Paganini. I'm sure of it. But first you must learn how to play the violin in sync with the soundtrack. Do you think you could do that?"

"Yes," Berl said. "I believe I could."

Berl's home in Beverly Hills surrounded by towering Royal Palm trees was a palatial estate purchased from a fading silent film star bankrupted by the introduction of talking pictures. His residence, the symbol of his stardom included a large swimming pool, a tennis court and a glass Hot

The Prodigy

House where his Japanese gardener cultivated Orchids, Frangipani, Bougainvillea and other exotic flowers. Every evening, after a long hard day at the studio, a day that began at dawn, Berl would sit and think about the eternal beauty of the one thing in his hectic life that would remain a joy forever. His flowers. His beautiful flowers. His only other recreation, steering a high-speed Stuz Bearcat sports car through the winding roads of the Hollywood Hills enabled him to escape the make-believe world he disliked. His favorite drive was an unpaved winding road on a mountain ridge overlooking the San Fernando valley where the snowcapped San Gabriel mountains looked down at the valley floor like sleeping giants. And when the yellow mustard flowered in Spring the Santa Barbara hills became a golden landscape delighting his eye and filling his heart with the desire to witness more beauty.

And certainly beauty is in the eye of the beholder. Driving along Hollywood's Wilshire Boulevard Berl looked up at a giant photograph of "Gentle Joe Tasma, Your Friendly Credit Dentist" smiling down from an enormous Billboard offering aspiring young movie stars the promising miracle of "The Hollywood smile". Sunset and Vine, "The Crossroads of America, The center of the World" lured hopeful "Starlets" who travelled to the Promised Land and invested their life's savings in careers that never materialized. Schwabs Pharmacy's crowded soda fountain was their Holy Grail where future Stars were miraculously discovered by Talent Scouts searching for that intangible quality known as "It". The belief a young nubile ingénue had "It" led to screen tests, contracts and too often the Casting Couch where every career opportunity had a price.

Berl had no need for the coercion of the Casting Couch. His virginity was overwhelmed by a series of encounters with women exploring his sexuality in ways far beyond his inexperienced imagination. He was a Star. A Star has power. And power is the greatest of all aphrodisiacs.

In the words of a celebrated song: Berl "learned the groundwork, the bouncing in bed work, and was told to take it from there." And he did indeed take all that was offered with the wild joy of a Novice released from the confines of vanished innocence. His numerous women were from all the races. All with pretty faces. Tall. Short. Thin. Fat. A cornucopia of undulating flesh that inflamed his loins with uncontrollable desire. And then, inevitably, Berl collapsed. After countless nights of revelry, his sexual appetite after a long day at work burned out his diminishing reserves of physical energy. His career suffered and he learned what a man would accomplish with his brain can be undone by his scrotum. Unbridled sex leads to nothing. It is unproductive. And outside of sex women are trouble.

At "The Pearly Gates", the main entrance to Berl's Studio, hundreds of Bobby Benson fans gathered twice a day seeking autographs. Security Guards controlling the screaming crowds enabled Berl to enter unharmed. Occasionally Berl stopped and signed his name exhilarated by the adoration that often resulted in clothing being torn from his body. Shirt tails, cuff links, and neckties were stolen in a wild adolescent frenzy of love. The price of celebrity. What every Star must sacrifice in return for success. Sightseeing Buses passing his Beverly Hills mansion with Star-struck tourists violated his privacy in a continuous parade of intruders. Yes, Berl thought, what can't be cured must be endured until the unendurable occurred when his parents, Riva and Jacob arrived at his door.

"You should have told us you were so unhappy." Jacob said reaching out to embrace Berl. "If we had known you were so troubled we would have done anything to accommodate you. You were the light of our life and the light of the world. But running away without a word, without so much as a hint how you felt was devastating. Your mother almost died of grief and Maestro Leonardo has never been the same. Without you his inspiration vanished. How you could do this to people who loved you?" Jacob turned away from his son wiping away tears with a large handkerchief. "It was Goldfarb's fault. He over-booked you. Squeezing every possible dollar from your hard work. Your great talent. It was too much. Too much. Too many hotels. Too many cities. Too many nights trying to sleep in a Pullman train. Sometimes I didn't know where we were or where we were going. Such a crazy life. But running away? That I don't understand."

Riva, Berl's mother began sobbing. "God gave you your genius because he made you a great artist," she explained. "To bring joy to the music lovers of this world and now you throw away this gift to be the All American Boy? I never thought I would ever be ashamed of you but that's what I was! Ashamed sitting there in the theater watching my son prance

130

across the screen with a simpering smile at everything your stupid girl friend said. Have you no shame? Movies are for the ignorant who know nothing of the finer things in life. Beauty! Truth! An appreciation of mankind's greatest achievement. Great Art! Movies degrade people who ask only for a mouthful of Popcorn and a few hours sitting in the dark watching their pathetic dreams come true. I don't understand how you can do this to yourself. To your parents who sacrificed their lives for your career!"

"And," Jacob demanded, "how are we supposed to live? For how many years we struggled, pinched pennies, did without, sacrificed everything to pay for your musical education. The finest teachers in the world you had and believe me they didn't come cheap. A fortune it costs to become a Child prodigy. And now you abandon us with no income. Leave us penniless. Destitute. How should we live I ask you. What will we have for when we are old? No son should ever do this to his parents. Not you my darling Berl. Not you."

Berl remained indifferent to his parent's agonized pleas. Standing in the doorway Jacob lowered his voice and asked plaintively: "Aren't you going to invite us in? It's not like we're strangers coming to your door like Beggars." Berl nodded and stepped aside as they entered the enormous hallway of his mansion. Jacob looked around at the grandeur. "Nu!" he said, shaking his head, admiring everything he saw. "Nu!" he said again. "I see you're doing all right by yourself. This is some Palace you got here!" Riva interrupted. "It's a dump," she said. "A vulgar ostentatious example of everything corrupting this country." Riva waved her arm in a sweeping disdainful gesture of contempt as she said: "This is nothing but conspicuous consumption. You should be ashamed to live like this when so many are starving. As if you didn't know we're having a depression." The Japanese Butler bowed to Berl's parents and carried their luggage into the house. Jacob followed, enjoying this show of deference as if he was the Lord of the Manor. "Well my boy," Jacob said affectionately, "I have nothing against a man being successful and letting the world know of his success. It's only human. You must be careful when you have money. You must be protected against everyone taking advantage of your innocent generosity. It's not easy being wealthy in a world filled with Con men and Advisors who will rob you blind. I should know. I've been taken more than once." Berl smiled and remained silent.

"What you need," Jacob said. "Is a Manager. Someone you can trust. Someone who will help you with your career pay your bills on time and make travel arrangements."

"I already have a Manager. A man I trust."

"Who is that?" Jacob asked. Disappointed.

"My Boss Mr. Pincus."

"He's not family," Jacob replied. "And only family you should trust with your money."

"I call him Papa," Berl explained, "and he knows what's good for my career. He's done more for me than anybody. The Studio's my family now."

On the first production day of "The lives and loves of Maestro Paganini" everyone agreed Berl was a natural for the part. Spontaneous talent flowed out of him and could not be suppressed. Through the magic of Make-up artists Berl's appearance was transformed from a young violin prodigy to a middle-aged virtuoso concertizing in all the great European Cities where he amazed audiences with his genius leaving behind a trail of broken-hearted lovers and unpaid gambling debts. As fame and fortune vanished, Berl's remorseful re-creation of Paganini's sad end brought tears to the eyes of the movie crew who wondered how someone so young could portray so much about life's inevitable tragedy. Papa Pincus was delighted. Watching the daily "Rushes" in his private theater confirmed his belief in Berl's future. Berl's fingering and bow arm movements perfectly synchronized with Play-Back music seemed a gift of the Gods! Expensive "re-takes" were rare. The mystery and wonder about his ability to play a violin virtuoso disappeared the day the Play-back tape recorder broke down. Refusing to allow an interruption in the production schedule Berl insisted the cameras keep rolling as he flawlessly played a live performance of a difficult Beethoven violin concerto. The astonished crew applauded. Overcome with gratitude the director embraced Berl kissing his hand. And learning what Berl had done, Papa Pincus rushed to his dressing room where Berl's make up was being removed and smiling, laughing said: "You never deceived me, my dear boy. Not for one minute did I not know who you really were. Fifteen years ago I heard you play at Carnegie Hall. An unforgettable experience. And believe me you haven't changed. Not at all. In my heart you will forever be the child prodigy who once made me cry for joy at the beauty you created."

"The Lives and Loves of Paganini" was a great success. Berl's career ascended into extravagant stardom where a Box Office King reigned and a thousand and one nights of sensual joy was rightfully his. A sadder and wiser Berl having fulfilled his appetite for meaningless sex indulged only in hard work appearing in two movies a year playing characters whose rise and fall from fame and fortune resembled Maestro Paganini's. Berl became the most talented voice at story conferences where his instinct for money-making scripts enabled him to produce successful films. At twenty-five, with full confidence in his young genius, Papa Pincus made Berl Executive Producer supervising all the studio's productions. Variety called Berl "Hollywood's Boy Wonder. The New Christ of Vine street". To his actors and directors Berl became a tyrant who was never wrong making or destroying promising careers with a phone call. And then, as it must come to all famous celebrities, the inevitable happened. Newspaper headlines reported every prurient detail of Paternity Lawsuits, filed by unscrupulous lawyers, confident their groundless claims will be settled to avoid destructive publicity during the years when the Legion of Decency had the power to bless or destroy a film's Box office earnings.

Maximilian Heister, better known as Mad Max, made paternity litigation a devious art form arousing the envy of more scrupulous members of the California Bar. Called "Dear Max" by grateful clients he diligently searched for pregnant litigants who could melt the hearts of Juries with proof their maternity resulted from sexual encounters with a famous Star. Whiplash and lower back pain lawsuits, despite his dramaturgical skill, lacked the conviction of love letters, hotel registrations and revealing photographs. Plaintiffs testifying in wheel chairs or strapped to a backboard lacked the tragic appeal of an innocent woman violated by lust. Max's courtroom performances were worthy of an Academy Award. His Paternity trials dramatized every salacious detail avidly reported by Journalists who increased their paper's circulation by writing incendiary headlines. Heartbreaking stories about the sins of the rich and famous enriched everyone except the Stars and Studios resigned to paying what was indeed criminal extortion.

Bubbles Bousquet, born Betty Bergen in a small Ohio farming town, was an ideal Litigant. A pathetic victim collapsing in the witness chair sobbing in response to Max Heister's carefully scripted dramatizations of her fate. Bubbles Bousquet was one of an expanding tribe of Hollywood's "Walking Wounded" working as a Drive-in Car Hop between occasional days as a movie Extra. Regularly unemployed, her acting career was supported carrying hamburgers, cheese burgers, cokes, French fries, and milkshakes and hooking the trays on car doors. Twenty four hour a day Drive-ins fed the insatiable hunger of a town that never slept. Bubbles enjoyed taking orders, laughing at customer's crude jokes, flirting, and wearing shorts and a drum majorette's costume emphasizing her attractive breasts and ass, she felt the feminine pleasure of being looked at by hungry eyes. When asked by lonely men "What time do you get off work?" she laughed and often replied: "My time is your time, if you make it worth something." Bubbles despised Sunset Boulevard Prostitutes soliciting drivers cruising the avenues for sex. Or late at night, knocking on Hotel room doors calling "John? John? John?" Bubbles never thought of herself as a "Hooker" taking on every horny slob at the Drive in. She never replied to drunks, or loudmouths parading their manhood. She preferred older men, sitting alone, politely ordering and after eating, anxious to talk. She knew how they felt, wanting someone to talk to more than a blow job. Living alone in her one bedroom apartment, waiting for her beauty and talent to be discovered, Bubbles learned loneliness and struggling to pay the rent was all the great Hollywood myth of Stardom offered. Bubbles never fought loneliness with drugs or alcohol. In crowded movie theaters her loneliness intensified. She felt she was born to live and die alone watching her life dissolve into nothingness. Lacking talent or gifts other than her beautiful body, Bubbles' Hollywood career followed the usual track of part-time Extra, Bit player, unemployable actress and "Party Girl" appearing at festivities where drugs, alcohol and recreational sex filled the days and nights of otherwise empty lives. Bubbles soon became part of the notorious "Hollywood Scene" that included murder, rape, accidental death by drowning, drug overdoses and high speed car accidents where photographs of the mangled bodies of the world's most beautiful people were page one news.

When questioned by Max Heister about his past relationship with Bubbles, Berl quietly and deliberately said: "I have no memory of ever having a relationship with Miss Bousquet."

Relentless Max Heister turned and smiled at the Jury dismissing Berl's denial. Then handing Berl a photograph he asked: "Study this and tell the Ladies and Gentlemen of the Jury what you see."

Berl glanced at the photograph a moment, nodded, and turning to the Jury replied: "My birthday party at Errol's Malibu Beach House." Max Heister smiled. "And is that you standing in the center of that photograph?"

"Yes," Berl said.

"And who else do you see in this picture?"

"Miss Bousquet," Berl replied.

"And when was that photograph taken?" Max Heister asked in a deep baritone voice.

"About six months ago," Berl replied. Max Heister turned to the Jury and said quietly: "Ladies and Gentlemen carefully note that the defendant stated this photograph was taken six months ago!" Holding up his left hand he slowly counted the fingers: "One… two… three… four… five!" Then raising his right hand he displayed one finger. "Five and one make six," he shouted triumphantly. "Five and one make six! Is that correct, sir?"

Berl nodded. 'Yes. Five and one make six."

Max Heister again turned to the Jury as if sharing this information with old friends said: "Six months is a very long time. Half a year I believe."

Berl nodded. "Yes," he replied.

Then, after a long moment of silence allowing the Jury time to consider this statement Max Heister walked to the witness table and standing next to Bubbles Bousquet placed a reassuring hand on her shoulder. "Ladies and Gentlemen of the Jury I submit for your consideration a sworn Affidavit from one of our nation's leading Gynecologists stating this unfortunate young lady has been carrying the defendant's unborn child for six months! Six months of worry. Six months of discomfort. Six months of uncertainty about how to pay bills resulting from a heartless unscrupulous moment of sexual pleasure by an irresponsible defendant who you must hold accountable for his transgressions." Pausing to allow his argument to be fully effective he handed a large handkerchief to a sobbing Bubbles Bousquet who delicately dried her tears.

"Oh! How the Mighty hath fallen!" Max Heister said in a mournful voice believing he was quoting the Bible. Oh! "How the mighty hath fallen. It grieves me to think this once paragon of manly virtue, this former inspiration to our youth, this All American Boy has betrayed everything decent citizens believe and live by. That is why I am asking you, ladies and gentlemen of the Jury, to defend our nation's honor by finding for the Plaintiff and demonstrating that Justice will always prevail in our beloved country!"

The sympathetic Jury found Berl guilty of Statutory Rape as Bubbles was a Minor. The outraged Judge ordered Child support payments until the unborn infant was twenty one and set payment for damages and Court costs at two hundred fifty thousand dollars.

Max Heister and his injured client were delighted. Berl and the Studio's Lawyers were outraged. And several weeks later, due to the trial's grief and strife Bubbles Bousquet miscarried.

EIGHT

Sylvia Angelo loved the sea. Every evening after a long workday she drove to the harbor to look at fishing boats and hear the seagulls cry as they fed on fish entrails discarded by fishermen who reminded her of her family in Monterey. Hard-working. Religious. And proud of their Italian heritage. At fourteen, Sylvia worked with other women in the Canary singing and laughing as they labored to relieve the drudgery of their lives. At eighteen she studied shorthand and touch-typing determined to escape a future that promised only marriage to a nice Italian boy and a lifetime growing fat raising six children.

Palm trees, warm sunshine and air perfumed by orange blossoms offered a happy alternative to Monterey's seasonal fogs and rain. Travelling south, staring out the window of a Greyhound bus, Sylvia marveled at the dramatic transition of the scenery to a benign desert climate thinking the City of Angels would soon acquire one more Angel. Sylvia Angelo did not dream of Hollywood stardom. Her remarkable short-hand speed and touch-typing skill promised more financial independence than that of an aspiring Starlet as Sylvia made a new life for herself. The Employment agency soon found her a job at Colossal Pictures where her reserved, modest and shy appearance confirmed her duties would be strictly secretarial. With hair combed back in a bun, wearing eyeglasses, her modest dresses demurely concealed a warm attractive body as yet undefiled.

The Prodigy

Pappa Pincus was delighted. Sylvia Angelo was exactly the young independent woman he admired. Self-supporting. Chaste. And above all, capable of being a wife able to properly raise an ideal All American family. Papa Pincus was also concerned about Berl's future. All work and no play could lead to another breakdown interrupting production for months. What Berl needed was a wife. Someone to come home to every evening. Someone to talk to and relieve the stress of his hard-driving life. Pappa Pincus picked up the phone and called the Studio's Secretarial Pool. Sylvia Angelo became Berl's Executive secretary and Pappa Pincus, leaning back in his upholstered chair smiled at the thought he was now Cupid.

Berl, rising from his desk and pacing around his office, dictated an endless stream of memos to all the studio's producers and department supervisors. Script revisions, casting and lighting, set and costume designs, music and recording problems and even the studio cafeteria were victims of his savage criticism. Sylvia Angelo's speed writing short-hand barely kept up with the blizzard of memos he dictated called "Snowflakes" by unhappy recipients who felt their professional abilities were being denigrated. For two hours every morning Sylvia transcribed Dictaphone discs recorded overnight by someone who never seemed to sleep. Variety called Berl "The Boy Wonder. The New Christ of Vine street" criticizing his repeated humiliation of celebrated authors and playwrights brought to Hollywood to enrich the artistic qualities of movies.

What kind of man is this? Sylvia Angelo wondered. Despised by so many? Without friends. And when his parents returned to New York he was glad to see them go. Alone, a solitary figure of power and authority seated behind an enormous bare desk with only a telephone and a memo pad for company. No photographs or paintings decorated his office walls. Only framed posters advertising productions he was proud of. His surrogate children, the only satisfactions of his barren life. Reading scripts, dictating memos, answering phone calls he seemed no more aware of Sylvia's presence than of the office furniture. All he knew of Sylvia was her ability to take dictation without asking him to repeat a sentence. He seemed a boy in a man's clothing playing at being a "Movie Mogul" living a script with no happy ending. Berl aroused Sylvia's pity. She knew enough to beware of pity for it can so easily be confused with love. And what is love? Sylvia wondered. What is this feeling pulling her down into the depths of emotions beyond her control? How could anyone love such a troubled man?

Berl's only passion, running the studio, absorbed all his time and energy. His only recreation living aboard his yacht operated by a professional Captain and crew cruising the Channel Islands off the Southern California coast when they weren't moored at a Long Beach dock. Sailing he recaptured the freedom he enjoyed roller skating remembering the wind in his face, the clouds overhead and the stars in the sky. The heat of the sun revived the vagabond feeling he enjoyed roller skating across the country fleeing his past. Aboard the yacht he felt like a wanderer again and not a prisoner laboring within studio walls that shut out the real world. Listening to the mournful cries of seagulls, inhaling the invigorating breath of the Pacific ocean, Berl had time to think and read. Not boring movie scripts but books. The ship's library fulfilled his hunger for what he had been deprived of by his parents. An education. Berl was embarrassed by his ignorance of knowledge beyond the demands of the classical music world. On weekends, away from the tyranny of telephones, telex messages and telegrams Berl did nothing but read. An eager voyager cruising the high seas of literature. Charles Dickens taught him about poverty, Mark Twain laughter at Man's folly, and Jack London the suffering of the poor. A voyage of discovery when he encountered Huckleberry Finn fleeing a barren life conforming to society's expectations. An Outcast with the moral courage to escape all conventions, Huckleberry Finn, like Berl, welcomed the challenge of experience. Good and bad. Kind and cruel. Discovering America, a boy becomes a man. A thinking man.

Berl wondered about the beauty and variety of the lives he encountered on his journey. The devout and the homeless, the rich and the poor, the despairing and the hopeful, the liars and the demagogues, the powerful and the powerless, the kind and the cruel, and those fortunate few who saw the world with seeing eyes and feeling hearts. Overcome by the joy of being alive Berl discovered what it was to witness mankind's savagery and fear knowing even God-fearing people are capable of unspeakable cruelty. Through reading Berl acquired fortitude becoming larger than himself learning life is an adventure in which the spirit makes a bargain with God. Berl's pity for mankind came later in a life redeemed by suffering.

Working aboard his yacht on weekends, Sylvia Angelo often accompanied Berl taking short-hand later transcribed for his attention when he returned to the studio Monday morning. Berl paced the deck with Sylvia struggling to record memos to subordinates. A remarkable flow of words from a man with a limited vocabulary.

"What is the word for someone who does something wrong?" Berl asked struggling with an elusive thought. Embarrassed by his ignorance.

Sylvia hesitated a moment. "Culprit, I believe."

Yes, that's right," Berl said gratefully. "A Culprit. Guilty as hell!" He resumed dictating and turning to look at Sylvia, nodded his appreciation. "You're better than a Dictionary," he said smiling.

Sylvia Angelo looked up from her notebook her face flushed at the unexpected compliment.

"There are so many words," Berl complained. "Too damn many. You don't need a lot of words for movies." He turned and stepped across the deck to the ship's rail staring out over the water at the blinking lights on the shoreline.

"Why do you say that?" Sylvia asked looking up from her notebook. "Movies can talk now."

Berl turned from the rail and faced her. "I think in pictures. Being uneducated isn't important." Sylvia Angelo laughed. Put down her notebook: "Do you want me to write that?"

"Hell no!" Berl said. "Just thinking out loud." He stared at Sylvia. Studying her face. Hesitating before asking: "What is the word for someone with no education?"

"Ignoramus," Sylvia replied. "An ignoramus."

"Berl nodded. "That's me all right. An ignoramus."

"But how can an ignoramus run a studio!" Sylvia argued.

"I work with fools. I'm King of the Fools!" He turned and looked out to sea. On shore a rotating light marked the harbor entrance. A Lighthouse horn blared mournfully.

Berl turned from the rail and walked to a table. He picked up a slice of bread. Returning to the boat's rail he tossed some bread overboard feeding seagulls circling overhead. The crying Gulls dove down catching the bread in mid-air. Berl shouted approval, joyfully throwing more bread into the air.

"At the studio I feed another kind of Gull begging me for attention. Feed them a mouthful a day and they're happy."

"Do you really believe that?"

"It's better to be feared than loved by Stars floating on thin air like Seagulls terrified they will someday come crashing down to earth with one flop. One destructive review."

"What a horrible way to live," Sylvia said. "Inhuman."

"There's no other way, Miss Angelo. No other way. With scandal-mongers Luella Parsons and Hedda Harper exposing every discretion Stars live in fear. I'm the only one shielding them from disaster paying off all the Jail Bait and San Quentin Quail in Hollywood."

"Jail Bait? San Quentin Quail?" Sylvia asked. What are you talking about?"

"Under-age Bimbos with hot pants. They're a dime a dozen in this town." Sylvia Angelo laughed. "So that's what makes you so unhappy running the studio."

"Happy? I do what has to be done. My job is no popularity contest."

Distracted by a mournful Seagull cry Berl looked up to watch the birds circling overhead. He turned to Sylvia and asked "Did you ever feed Seagulls?"

"Yes."

"Where?"

"Monterey harbor."

"Made you feel good?"

"Yes."

"Free as a bird?"

"Yes. And happy," Sylvia explained.

"Never knew much about happiness," Berl confessed, recalling his past. "I don't remember ever feeling free as those birds."

Sylvia remained silent. Her face suddenly saddened by his revelation.

"Most people I know are miserable, unhappy," Berl continued.

"Not everybody," Sylvia insisted.

"Not you? You're not unhappy?"

"No."

"Why is that?"

"I enjoy my work." Berl nodded, thinking a moment about her reply. "Is this job all you want out of Life?"

"No," Sylvia replied. "I want much more. But that will come with time."

"You really believe that?"

"Yes."

"Then you're a fool. Only fools believe in happiness." Berl turned away from the ship's rail to stare at Sylvia. A long questioning look before asking: "Do you ever get seasick Miss Angelo?"

"Never."

"That's good," Berl replied, nodding approval. "Next weekend we're sailing to Catalina Island. A boat rots at a dock."

"Why is that?" Sylvia asked.

"Moored in one place too long is no good." Surprised at the invitation Sylvia Angelo hesitated. Berl smiled a reassuring smile.

"Nothing better than a change of scenery when working hard."

"Yes, that's true," Sylvia replied. "There's must be more to life than hard work."

"Believe me, Miss Angelo, there is. Much more."

Berl smiled at Sylvia. A paternal smile. "You're a child Miss Angelo. A beautiful innocent child. Life hasn't destroyed your innocence. I don't think you ever been caught in a trap, abused by people you loved. Known despair."

"I've had my bad moments." Berl turned to Sylvia. His face anguished. "You could never believe what my childhood was like, Miss Angelo. A Child Prodigy giving concerts around the world to support my parents. Thirty, forty a year, always travelling, hotels my only home. No education. Only a cruel and unrelenting discipline instead of love. I hated that life. My only friend was another Prodigy who was also abused by his parents."

"I'm sorry to hear that," Sylvia replied sympathetically. "Losing your love of life is a kind of death."

"Worse than death," Miss Angelo. "The dead feel no pain. No anguish. I even thought of suicide until something wonderful happened that saved my life. Berl paused as if reluctant to confess. Remembering. "One day, at the most miserable time in my life I opened my violin case and found a beautiful hand-written note from Menahim, my dearest and only friend. I broke down. Began to cry. Sobbing my heart out because I now had a reason to live.

"What did the note say?"

"I love you."

Mournful crying Seagulls recalled Sylvia Angelo's memory of Cannery Row where every afternoon after school she fed the Seagulls. She remembered her boyfriend Leon who shared her joy watching birds swoop down to catch chunks of bread before they disappeared beneath the water. Tall and handsome, Leon had dark olive skin Sylvia loved to caress, their adolescent love only consummated when alone with their dreams. And what dreams they had Sylvia remembered. Dreams of lives they would have had if Leon had lived. Leaning over the edge of the pier throwing bread into the air, Leon fell into the water. Unable to swim he was carried out to sea by swift currents that ripped out a piece of her heart. Sylvia vowed to never love again. Never again suffer the pain of being separated from happiness. Her recurring dreams were cruel. One night, dreaming of taking Communion in a flowing white wedding dress, Sylvia lifted her veil and turned to look for Leon who was never there. She awoke sobbing, mourning her loss. Working long hours in the Cannery, and with the healing powers of time, Sylvia dreamt of renewing her life where sunshine and Palm trees replaced the cold fog and rain of Monterey. In Los Angeles Sylvia's sorrow diminished as she acquired hope by thinking I want to fall deeply, truly in love. Is that too much to ask?" She wondered. "Was this an impossible dream?"

Berl seemed driven by demons banished by engaging with enemies who can only be defeated by working longer hours dictating more memos. Only through hard work would Berl rediscover who he really was.

One afternoon on the boat, Berl paused while dictating asking: 'Where you ever happy as a child, Miss Angelo?"

"Yes," Sylvia replied.

"Why do you say that?" he asked.

"We always had a place to live. Food to eat." she said.

"Is that all?" Berl asked. "I had four brothers and two sisters. My parents were alive."

"A family."

"Yes. A family."

Berl turned and walked to the ship's rail and looked out to sea. "I've often wondered what it would be like to have a family."

"Noisy. Crowded. Full of life," Sylvia replied.

"You've been fortunate, Miss Angelo."

"And so have you. You have had everything you want."

Berl laughed. Turned to face Sylvia. Hesitating. Speaking quietly he said: "You'll never know what it's like having nothing you really want, Miss Angelo. Nothing you truly value. I was given everything I didn't want and when I discovered the truth about my life it almost killed me." Sylvia remained silent. Closed her notebook. She hesitated before slowly turning to look at Berl. She shook her head. "You poor man," she said quietly. Her voice trembling. "You poor man."

"Poor little rich boy is what you mean," Berl replied. "Poor little rich boy."

When Sylvia first met Berl she thought she was looking at a portrait of a young man of breathtaking beauty. A gentle smile and clear radiant eyes revealed an unblemished soul showing the wonder of being young and alive anticipating the future. Then, slowly, with time, visible changes occurred. His smile became cynical, his lips pressed together in an uninviting grin. His face aged, the appearance she once found attractive vanished. Sylvia now wrote his dictation staring down at her notebook. Remembering her first meeting she avoided looking at the face of an angry man she once saw as the "Boy Wonder".

"The face is the mirror of the soul," her father once explained, "the face reveals the Man. And every man is responsible for what he looks like."

Sylvia Angelo enjoyed sitting in a darkened room in her apartment appreciating a quiet evening after taking dictation all day. She filled her lonely hours reading and listening to Italian Opera. Performers dying for love brought tears to her eyes, and when their suffering overwhelmed her tender feelings she broke down and sobbed. From Opera Librettos Sylvia Angelo learned to be careful who she loved. Leon's death was her first encounter with tragedy. Looking in a mirror she searched for evidence of pain. Sorrowful eyes. Lines of despair. But alas, the mirror reflected hope and beauty. Someone radiant with life. And after months working with Berl he became different pacing back and forth like a caged animal, head down, dictating in a harsh voice. The beautiful boy was gone. Berl's eyes narrowed, became hooded projecting ruthless power. A "Movie Mogul" contemptuous of all he governed. Clearly not someone to get involved with. Sylvia recognized the danger of loving Berl. Beware of pity, she told herself as she resisted a power beyond her control.

One day Berl asked: "What was life like in Monterey, Miss Angelo?"

"Very ordinary."

"What do you mean by ordinary?"

"I had a father, mother, brothers and sisters. Aunts, Uncles, Cousins. A real Italian family."

"Like in the movies?"

"Yes."

"Audiences love family pictures."

"They're not real," Sylvia replied. "Not real at all."

"They don't have to be." Berl replied. "Audiences pay to see lives better than what they have. Makes them feel good." He turned and faced

Sylvia. Suddenly quiet he said: "I want you to know, Miss Angelo, I enjoy working with you."

"Thank you."

"My comment is strictly professional."

"Of course."

"This town is full of Bimbos screwing their way to stardom. A young lady is rare. I don't have to worry you're gonna some day sue me. Colossal Pictures has no casting couch. One transgression and you're through."

"That's reassuring."

"Have you ever been in love, Miss Angelo?"

"Yes."

"When was that?"

"Many years ago."

"What happened?"

"The boy died."

"I'm sorry to hear that."

"Yes."

"I've been in love. Or thought I was. Many times," Berl confessed.

"What happened?"

"Heart break. Disappointment. Hope I never fall in love again." Sylvia smiled, nodded, and laughing said: "That's how I feel."

"Good," Berl replied extending his hand in agreement. "We'll stay out of trouble. Have nothing to worry about."

"Go West young man, Go West and grow up with the country!" wrote Horace Greeley Editor of the New York Tribune in 1836. The West is the true destination for young Americans," he advised inspiring hundreds of thousands of Emigrants to cross the trackless Prairies and forbidding deserts on foot or in covered wagons creating a new nation. Their westward trek ended when they arrived at the shores of the Pacific ocean. Homesteaders fulfilled their expectations by hard work, and devotion to the principals of Liberty and justice for all. Here they founded California. And here in the golden state, Berl's participation in the great American dream continued, including weekends on his yacht exploring wild Pacific shores with Sylvia Angelo. Visiting the Channel islands, inhabited only by sea lions, seals, sea otters, bald eagles and grey whales, they discovered an America of strange kelp forests and tidal pools in an extraordinary wildlife refuge preserved as a National Park. Sylvia delighted in going to sea. Being a part of something primeval. Unchanged since the beginning of time. A delighted Berl commented: "You have great sea legs. Never sick."

"I'm a fisherman's daughter," Sylvia explained. "And so you went fishing?" Sylvia nodded and smiled. "Ate so much Tuna our stomachs went in and out with the tide."

"And that made you a Mermaid?"

Sylvia laughed, shaking her head. "Mermaids can't take dictation. They have no fingers."

"Well," Berl confessed, "I'm no sailor. Most happy when tied up to a dock."

"Running aground on Champagne bottles."

"Everything's possible."

"Like what?"

"Like falling in love."

"I thought we agreed not to."

"A gentlemen's agreement."

"So?" Sylvia asked.

"I'm no gentleman."

Sylvia shook her head. Disagreed. "You're not what I remember in High school where I needed three arms to fend off the boys when their hormones where raging."

"I've never been to school," Berl confessed. "know nothing about that."

"Never dated a girl?"

"Never. I was home schooled by my parents."

"Well, you didn't miss much. I learned the facts of life working in the Cannery."

"Like what?"

"Like there's good people in this world. Honest hardworking people."

"Where I lived we didn't know our neighbors," Berl said.

"Then you don't know anything about people," Sylvia replied. "There's all kinds, good and bad. And you must know one from the other to survive."

"Well you're doing more than just survive."

"That's right," Sylvia replied. "This town is hard on girls. It's feel touch and grab and cover your breasts wherever you go. Women are common property available to all. Everybody's somebody they're not. A costume party where lust is confused with love and nothing's real. I'm lucky. Pappa Pincus runs the studio like a Sunday school."

"He believes in the Golden Rule."

"Do onto others as you would have them do unto you."

"Not a bad idea," Berl said. "But not practical. In Hollywood it's do unto them before they do it to you."

"The Law of the Jungle," Sylvia commented.
"So where do you think you are? Berl asked.
"Paradise?"

"It could be," Sylvia replied. "Hollywood's got everything. Sunshine, Palm trees, Mountains, ocean beaches. What more could you ask for?"

"Better people," Berl replied. "All our misfits, losers and dreamers come here bringing their pathetic tragedies with them."

"All they want is a better life," Sylvia said. "Why I left Monterey.

"And have you found a better life here?"

"I think so," Sylvia replied. "I think so."

"And what is a better life"

"Being free to come and go as you please. Wake up in the morning anticipating what the day will bring. Every one a fresh beginning. Some days my heart's so full, I'm so happy I sing and dance around my room. My neighbors complain. Think I'm going mad. And maybe I am. Never felt this way working in a fish Cannery."

"You're a remarkable woman Sylvia," Berl said. "Most remarkable. I've never felt that way myself."

"Why not? Why not let yourself go and be happy? You're working yourself to death for what? More money? A bigger yacht? What's your life all about?"

"I don't know."

"Even a famous Movie Mogul is entitled to some happiness."

"I agree. But how? I have my responsibilities."

"Yes you do!" Sylvia insisted. "But what do you owe yourself?" She demanded. "A heart attack? A fancy funeral crowded with mourners glad to see you go? A full page Obituary in Variety? Is that all you want? Because if it is, that's what you'll get."

Berl walked to the ship's rail and looked out to sea pausing a moment before turning to Sylvia. Hesitating. Smiling. Almost pleading, he said: "Teach me to dance, Sylvia. Teach me to dance." Surprised at his request Sylvia asked: "You've never danced with a girl?"

"Never."

"Well you need music," she explained, walking to a record player selecting a record. There's Benny Goodman, Tommy Dorsey, and Guy Lombardo. Who is your favorite?"

"I don't know much about that kind of music, Miss Angelo."

"Never heard of them?"

"Never."

"Well when dancing you listen to what they're playing. Hear the beat of the music as you hold your partner in your arms swaying back and forth like you're out of this world."

"Out of this world?" Berl asked. How's that possible?"

"Believe me it can happen," Sylvia responded. "It's like when dancing you go so deep into each other's hearts the two of you become one."

Berl hesitated. Then reached out taking Sylvia in his arms he began moving in time to the music's slow pulsating beat. Nodding. Filled with the pleasure of the moment he said: "I think I'm going to enjoy dancing with you, Miss Angelo."

Sylvia Angelo loved dawn at sea. Watching the rising sun burn off the early morning mists stimulated clear thinking as she confronted the reality of her life. Like ships groping through a fog, they were aware of danger, avoiding coming together. Rejecting intimacy. They were friends. Companions. Never lovers. To prevent being hurt, Berl distanced himself from Sylvia. Receiving but not returning love. Her love. In a world offering possibilities of renewal Berl remained the hungry child who fled his past. Cold. Unfeeling. Insensitive. Berl grew more remote as if being unmarried was what he wanted. Sylvia Angelo respected his wishes accepting the situation, destined to be no more than a sea-going secretary, a companionable shipmate. Sylvia Angelo learned early in life the ocean can be a kind friend or a ferocious enemy. Listening to the thundering surf pounding California's magnificent coastal beaches bringing ashore the Flotsam and Jetsam of distant lands, she witnessed with awe and humility the power and majesty of the sea. For generations the Angelo's lived and thrived as fishermen knowing what has been given can be taken away. What the sea gives, it can reclaim. Savage and unforgiving, the ocean's winds and currents are more powerful than anything on earth and have never been conquered. Sylvia's passion for swimming, embracing her inheritance like a lover became a daily ritual of discovery with every plunge into the surf. At the end of a day taking dictation, Sylvia Angelo climbed down the ship's swim ladder and dove into the sea. The friendly sea. Her other home where weightless, as if floating in space her arms propelled her through the water, her head turning, mouth opening to inhale the sharp salty tang of sea air. Sylvia felt herself belong to the sea, a marine creature returning to the source of all life. Swimming up-current from the yacht to insure an easy downstream return to the boarding ladder, every stroke brought her closer to where she could relax, turn around and let the currents carry her back to the boat. Reaching the farthest point of safe return, exhausted from swimming for an hour against a treacherous force, Sylvia discovered the tide had reversed the flow of the currents she must now swim against to survive. And so what the sea gave it soon reclaimed.

For five days, from early morning to sunset, Berl searched the seas around Catalina Island looking for Sylvia Angelo. Standing in the bow of his yacht, blinded by the sun's dazzling glare on unforgiving waters, Berl refused to abandon hope somehow, somewhere Sylvia would be found. The yacht searched beaches, tidal pools and floating Kelp forests following the ocean's turbulent currents as Berl insisted they not leave Sylvia's remains to sharks. When they returned to the Long Beach dock to refuel, the Captain dismissed Berl's demand they continue as futile. "The sea does not always surrender its dead," he explained. "What the sea gives it reclaims."

Sleepless nights were torment. In the dark hours of his sorrow Berl descended into the Devil's purgatory of what might have been. Of what he failed to respond to. Of what he dismissed. Of what will never come again for Sylvia is no more. He had been blind, he quietly sobbed. Never again would he receive the love of a good woman. A woman awakening his long dormant ability to return love.

The Prodigy

For many days, seated in a deck chair, he stared out to sea as if expecting Sylvia to reappear, to emerge from the depths of his despair to banish pain. Waiting for him at the dock, crowds of "Legion of Decency" demonstrators held signs protesting another Hollywood "Love Boat Tragedy" where a "Movie Mogul and his Mistress" learned "The Wages of Sin are Death". Reporters and Newsreel cameramen, restrained by the Police, shouted rude questions as Berl stepped off his yacht to escape the tumult. Grey-haired Long Beach Garden club women pounded his limousine's windows hysterically shouting "Shame! Shame! Shame!" as Berl raised his hands to his ears, shutting his eyes as if to banish a vision of a future of unbearable misery.

Everything about Big John Balboa was large. Six foot four, 260 pounds, two oversized hands that looked like shovels, Big John worked his way through Law School wrestling every Saturday night at the Los Angeles Coliseum. Cheering audiences, swilling beer and eating popcorn, loved his violent throw-downs, body slams, head butts and Tarzan jungle yells heard out in the street by enthusiastic crowds without the price of admission to a professional wrestling match. Also enormous was Big John's political ambitions recognizing the way to the Governor's mansion often began in a Prosecutor's office. The three previous Governors started their political careers as Prosecutors, and campaigning as a dedicated fighter in the "War on Crime" John Balboa easily defeated "Soft-on-

Crime" opponent Bobby Bruce by calling him "Turn 'em loose Bruce".

Convicting Berl, "The Hollywood Boy Wonder" of defiling young virgins, making him responsible for Sylvia Angelo's disappearance, John Balboa believed would advance his political career. A show-trial covered by newsreel cameras and journalists from around the world would make Balboa's name as recognizable as the stars whose sexual transgressions shocked Puritanical America. Ruined lives and careers, humiliation, shame and disgrace were the high price of Hollywood celebrity and John Balboa demanded Jail time for Berl as well as the Legion of Decency condemnation that drove Charlie Chaplin out of the country for liaisons with adolescent girls. Statuary Rape, impairing the morals of a Minor convictions were not difficult for a Prosecutor trying to convince a conservative California Jury.

"EQUAL JUSTICE UNDER LAW" was a pledge carved in stone above the County Court House door. For Big John Balboa, this promise raised the question: "what is Equal Justice?" In a Judicial system of pliable Grand Juries where Court Reporters believed "Balboa could indict a ham sandwich", Equal Justice was whatever Balboa believed it to be. His Jury selections eliminated all but "Born again Christians", Parents with teen-age daughters, and Red, White and Blue Patriots defending our nation's virtue. To hold the world spellbound for months, perhaps years, a trial must tell a compelling story. With no witnesses to Silvia's disappearance, without a recovered body for a Forensic report, Sylvia's story was written by headline-seeking journalists guided by John Balboa's narrative of events no one had ever seen. "Please identify yourself for the Jury," Big John Balboa asked in a commanding voice.

Berl leaned forward in his seat replying quietly, "My name is Berl Baron." The Prosecutor shook his head unhappily, asking: "Speak louder, sir, I don't think everyone heard you." Turning to the Jury, in a stronger voice Berl replied: "My name is Berl Baron."

"I mean your real name!" John Balboa insisted. Raising his voice impatiently.

"My legal name is Berl Baron," Berl repeated, attempting to comply.

"I mean the name you were born with!" the Prosecutor said. Your parent's name."

Berl shifted in his chair. Still grieved by his loss. Confused. "I don't understand what you want. I no longer use their name," he said quietly. "So you changed your name," the Prosecutor said sarcastically. "We're you ashamed of your true, real, family name?"

"No!" Berl insisted. "There were too many letters for a Theater marquee. No room for long names."

"And so tell us that very long name you no longer use?"

"Baronofsky," Berl replied. "For the benefit of a Jury unfamiliar with foreign names would you please spell it?" Balboa demanded. Berl hesitated, thought for a moment and then replied. "B...A...R...O...N...O...F...S...K...Y."

"And how does a simple God-fearing American pronounce such a name?" Balboa asked.

"Baronofsky," Berl replied quietly.

"What sort of a name is that?" the Prosecutor said walking to the Jury box shaking his head.

"A Russian name. My parents were born in Russia."

"And where were you born?" Balboa asked.

"In Brooklyn, New York, In a hospital."

"And when were you Baptized or confirmed in some religious faith?" Balboa demanded. "Never," Berl replied. "My parents were not very religious."

"Were they Atheists? Non-believers?" Balboa continued as if shocked by the response. "Were your parents Godless?"

"No! No! I wouldn't say that," Berl insisted. "They just weren't religious."

"And you?" Balboa asked raising his voice. "What Faith do you profess?" Several excited jurors coughed. Leaned forward in their chairs. One sipped a cup of water. Balboa waited for quiet before continuing. "I ask you again, what religion do you believe in?"

"Well, I don't know. I've never been in a Synagogue or a Church."

"Never?" Balboa asked.

"Never," Berl replied.

"Well," Balboa said pretending disbelief. You seem to have been raised in Godless Russia where the sanctity of Holy Matrimony has been replaced by an abomination called Free Love!"

Berl shook his head, unable to reply. He turned in his chair asking the Judge for guidance who smiled and said: "Answer the Prosecutor's question."

"What can I say," Berl protested, "to such a stupid accusation?"

Outraged, Balboa shouted: "Do you believe in God?"

"I don't know," Berl replied. "I've often thought about him."

"When was that?" Balboa demanded. "When did you think about God?"

Berl hesitated a moment. Remembering. "When I saw him." Balboa stepped forward to rest his hands on the edge of the witness box. Speechless, incredulous, in a reverent voice asked: "You saw God?"

Berl nodded. "Many times."

"And when did these miraculous visions occur?"

"Well" Berl replied quietly, remembering. "Mornings with the sun burning off the mist seeing the countryside with birds singing and everything pure and fresh makes you wonder how all this happened? This beauty most people never notice. And traveling in the wind and the rain it's hard to explain who made this world? It's so big! So enormous! So mysterious! Could it be God?"

"Is that what you saw?" Balboa asked, trembling. "Nothing else?"

"What more can there be?" Berl answered the Prosecutor. "What more can there be? Only God can make a tree, you know."

"PHILANDERING MOVIE MOGUL SAW GOD!!!" screamed headlines in the Los Angele Times. VARIETY, the movie industry's Trade Journal asked: "Has Hollywood's most notorious Walking Penis had a revelation?" Big John Balboa was pleased. Berl would convict himself with his incredible testimony.

"Tell me about your relationship with Miss Bousquet," Balboa demanded.

"I never had a relationship with Miss Bousquet," Berl insisted.

"You were the father of her child," the Prosecutor continued.

"An outrageous lie!" Berl shouted. "No Blood Test. No evidence of paternity. I never met Miss Bousquet."

"Yet your employer paid several hundred thousand dollars to atone for your flagrant disrespect for all the conventional rules of a civilized society."

"My trial was extortion. A shake down. A pay-off to someone willing to lie about something that never happened."

"Your Lawyers accepted the Judgment."

"To protect the Studio's good name. They make family pictures."

"And what about your good name?" the Prosecutor asked. "Do you believe you can rehabilitate your reputation with money?"

"No," Berl replied. "There's no such thing as Truth. Or any interest in what is true or false. A liar, a lawyer and a compliant Jury can easily destroy a lifetime of good work. My good name, my most precious possession can be ruined because I'm vulnerable to anyone willing to accuse me of anything."

"You've never done anything wrong?" asked the Prosecutor smiling sarcastically.

"I didn't say that," Berl replied. "All I am saying is that Truth has little chance of being heard in this town, in this Courtroom. All I am saying is give Truth a chance!"

The next day Jurors studied the enlarged photographs of a now infamous yacht. The Prosecutor, holding a lecturer's pointer turned and asked Berl: " For the benefit of our Jury would you please indicate where you were at the time Miss Silvia Angelo disappeared."

Berl took the pointer locating his stateroom. "And what were you doing at that time?"

"Sleeping. After a long day dictating memos I was exhausted."

"And where were the Captain and crew?"

"Ashore. At Avalon."

"Doing what?"

"Gambling at the Casino."

"Then you were alone. No one else on board?"

"Yes."

"And where was Miss Angelo?"

"Taking her afternoon swim. Unwinding after a long hard day at work. She loved swimming."

Retrieving the Pointer, the Prosecutor stepped to the photographs and asked. "Was it safe to anchor such a large yacht with only the owner on board?"

"Very safe. Avalon is a sheltered harbor."

"Then you didn't send the Captain and crew ashore?"

"Certainly not," Berl insisted.

"And when Miss Angelo returned from her swim and you awoke what then?

"We had a Sundowner."

"A Sundowner?" Balboa asked startled by Berl's response.

"Yes. Best time of the day sitting there watching a beautiful sunset. I'd have some Smironoff Vodkas while Sylvia enjoyed a glass of wine."

"Russian Vodka?" asked the Prosecutor raising his hand as if holding a glass.

"Yes. Very smooth. Especially with Caviar." The Prosecutor smiled admiring his response. He turned to another large photograph and paused pointing at it dramatically. "Please tell the Jury what they are looking at."

"The stern of my yacht," Berl replied. "What sailors call the aft end or rear of a boat."

"Yes."

"Take a good close look and tell me if you see anything in this photograph that should be there. Something missing."

"There's no swim ladder."

"And what is a swim ladder? What vital purpose does it serve?" the Prosecutor demanded.

"For going into the water and climbing back aboard again."

"And how is it secured to the boat?"

"Hooked over the stern rail."

"You mean it just hangs there?" The Prosecutor asked shaking his head. Incredulous.

"It is tied down by a good strong line to a deck cleat," Berl replied.

"A good strong line? Then please explain why this photograph taken just after Miss Angelo was reported missing shows no swim ladder?"

"I can't explain that."

"And if, after a long hard swim, Miss Angelo returned unable to climb back aboard your yacht what would she do?"

"Call for help."

"And at that tragic moment of life or death where would you be?"

"In my stateroom. Sleeping."

"You wouldn't hear her cry for help?"

"No."

The Jury shuffled their feet, coughed, sipped water and leaned forward to get a better look at the photograph. Some shook their heads in disbelief. The Prosecutor paused a moment before demanding: "You heard nothing? No shouting or screaming of a young beautiful woman fighting for her life?"

"No!" Berl cried out. Sobbing. "I heard nothing! Nothing!"

An angry Juror shouted an obscenity. The Judge pounded his gavel calling for order as Berl struggled for composure. The Prosecutor handed Berl a handkerchief. "I have a few more questions that will explain what happened. So be patient and answer truthfully. Was Miss Angelo pregnant?"

"No! No!" Berl shouted. "We were never lovers! Never!" Sobbing, he pressed the handkerchief to his face wiping away tears.

Sympathetic. Understanding, the Prosecutor asked: "Was Miss Angelo in love with you?"

"I believe so."

"And were you in love with Miss Angelo?"

"Yes. Yes. Although I didn't know how much I loved her until now."

"And you never considered marrying Miss Angelo despite the fact she was carrying your child?"

"There's no way she could be pregnant. We never slept together! Never!"

166

"There was never one moment of illicit passion? Not one moment when overpowered by lust you took advantage of Miss Angelo?"

"That never happened! Never!"

"And in a heartless attempt to evade another expensive Paternity lawsuit you cut the lines securing the swim ladder to the boat! Tell the truth! The whole truth! And nothing but the truth! Isn't that what really happened? Isn't that what you planned? Isn't that what you did to escape your responsibility to a beautiful woman who had her life taken away by your ungodly lust?"

Without a corpse, death certificate or eye-witness, the Judge and Jury considered ten to fifteen years for Manslaughter the only legally permissible penalty for Berl's alleged crime. With his reputation as a "War on Crime" fighter now dramatically enhanced, Big John Balboa's path to the Governor's Mansion was paved with lurid headlines and hysterical radio broadcasters mesmerizing thoughtless and uneducated Jurors.

"Who cut the swim ladder rope" remained an unsolved mystery. That Sylvia Angelo ever overcame the deadly ocean currents and returned to the boat is known only to God.

NINE

San Quentin Correctional facility overlooking San Francisco Bay incarcerated 3000 prisoners according to behavior. Open perimeter Level One dormitories accommodated the most trustworthy while in Level Two armed guards patrolled barbed wire fences. San Quentin also housed our nation's most populous Death Row where between 1893 and 1937 two hundred fifteen convicted murderers, rapists and sex offenders were hung. There was also an "Adjustment Center" where after five years in solitary confinement the famous "Dungeon Man" established a national record for punishment that did not fit the crime.

Free of the exhausting burden of managing a large movie studio Berl quickly adjusted to a daily routine of eating, sleeping and exercising in the Prison yard. Telephone calls, story conferences, screenings and critical decisions that formerly occupied his working day were not missed. In prison he felt he had escaped another breakdown. Another "burnout" following the death of his beloved friend Menahim. And with Sylvia gone he could grieve free of the media's insatiable appetite for lurid publicity. This new freedom reminded him of roller skating across the country his mind free to wander. Free to think and feel. Free of the burden of a "Movie Mogul's" emotionally barren life. Free to finally come to rest and be himself discovering who and what he truly was as a human being. Who am I?

What am I"? What am I to become? were questions
he tried to answer. And so Berl thought about the
circumstances of a life that granted him the great gift
of freedom only inside a prison wall. With time to
read, the Prison Library exposed his ignorance, his
lack of education and returning to his cell after a day
at the Prison Farm, he read while other prisoners
exercised or played baseball. Pappa Pincus died of a
broken-heart promising Berl he would resume his
career when free. Abandoned by Hollywood,
without family or friends, without letters or visitors,
past, present and future became timeless. A blank
calendar. Days weeks and months unaccounted for.
For someone once ruled by the clock, Time was now
without meaning he would live his life in Limbo.

While being escorted to the Visitor's Hall Berl
could not imagine who would ask to see him. He
refused all press and radio interviews and certainly
his parents disowned him. Looking through the wire
screen barrier separating him from his visitor Berl
saw a dignified old Fisherman with a strong deeply
lined and weathered face surprisingly sympathetic.

"I'm Captain Angelo," the visitor said, nodding
a gentle smile. "Sylvia's father."

Berl hesitated, shaking his head before replying,
"I'm sorry for your loss, Captain Angelo. Very sorry."

Captain Angelo leaned forward in his chair
almost pressing his face against the screen. "I know
that Mr. Baron," he said, "I'm certain of that."

Confused. Not knowing what to say Berl asked,
"Why are you here Captain Angelo?"

The old man paused and again nodded. "I've
come to tell you I know you did not kill Sylvia. I'm

sure you are innocent. I could not stay in Monterrey sitting on my boat thinking about you here for something you did not do. I asked myself what would Sylvia want me to do?"

"I thank you for your visit Captain Angelo."

"A great injustice!" the old man said raising his voice. "A great injustice! I don't see how Sylvia can rest in peace If I don't come and show you what she wrote." Captain Angelo raised his hand holding a bundle of letters tied in a small blue ribbon.

"And what did she write?" Berl asked.

"That she truly loved you."

"I know that now, Captain Angelo. I know that now."

"With all her heart and soul she loved you and so you must be a good man for Sylvia to love you like that."

Berl remained silent looking through the screen fighting back tears as he stared at the letters on the other side of the barrier. He reached out attempting to touch them.

Captain Angelo held out his hand. "I've brought you her letters, Mr. Baron. Beautiful letters she wrote asking my permission to marry outside our faith. She told me what a good man you are. What a good husband you would be and I would someday be proud to have you in our family. You see we are a very proud family Mr. Baron. Only good people. No murderers! No never!"

Berl shifted in his seat. He turned and looked up at the wall clock grateful the visit would soon end.

Captain Angelo held up the letters. "I want you to have Sylvia's letters. You should read them."

Berl shook his head fighting back tears. "I don't want the letters Captain Angelo."

Captain Angelo raised the letters in his two hands offering the gift of Sylvia's love like a Priest elevating the Host. "Why not, Mr. Baron. Why in God's name can you not want to read her beautiful words?"

"I don't think I could survive more pain, Captain Angelo. I'm not that strong."

"I will leave the letters with the Guard," Captain Angelo insisted. "He will give them to you."

"Please don't," Berl pleaded. "I'm trying to forget."

"Forget?" Captain Angelo shouted, shaking his head. "Forget?" he asked. "How can you forget Sylvia? How can you not remember such beauty, such love?"

"Remembering is driving me mad, Captain Angelo. Remorse is cruel and endless."

"Memories are all I have, Mr. Baron. Beautiful memories I must hold on to if I am going to go on living. Memories can not be discarded like old clothes. Memories are my most precious possession. What keeps me alive!"

Big Jim was an old-time "Lifer" incarcerated for a rape he did not commit. At lunchtime at the prison farm shaded under a canvas tarp, Big Jim told his story. His Odyssey. "Innocent as a new born babe and they found me guilty," he said. "When I refused to marry her she accused me of rape! Her word against mine and they believed her! I tell you women are the Devil's candy and so what can't be cured must be endured and that's what I'm doing in this life. Endure! Endure! Endure!"

Big Jim was also a "Trustee" supervising convicts at the Prison Farm. Six feet four, broad shouldered, his deep baritone voice and laughter were heard throughout the Prison yard every Sunday morning when he served as an itinerant Preacher. Clapping hands, calling out to his congregation, he brought joy and religious fervor to wretched prisoners serving their time on the edge of despair.

Gathering his congregation around him, summoned by the incessant beat of Gospel song, he sang: "We are climbing Jacob's ladder!" Raising and waving his arms pointing to the heavens he cried: "We are climbing Jacob's Ladder! We are climbing Jacob's ladder!" His congregation clapped hands shouting "Higher and higher! Higher and higher!" Big Jim nodded, his body swaying to the beat: "Yes! Yes! Yes!" he said "Higher and Higher! Higher! and Higher!" When the worshippers' emotions peaked he shouted: "We are the soldiers of the Lord! We are the soldiers of the Lord!" Concluding his sermon Big Jim sang in the slow rhythms of an ancient hymn: "There is a balm in Gilead to heal the sin-sick soul, there is a balm in Gilead to make the wounded whole!"

"To heal the sin-sick soul. To make the wounded whole" were more than words for Berl rising from despair. They held out hope and the expectation of future possibilities. His friendship with Big Jim was the balm in Gilead for Berl.

Berl enjoyed working the Prison Farm. Plowing, seeding, chopping the soil with a hoe, he developed an attachment to Mother Earth coming from hard backbreaking work. He felt he belonged to something previously unknown. As the crops ripened he knew the joy of creating something of essential value. Food he planted and grew and would eat.

Big Jim came to him one morning and asked: "Show me your hands." Berl put down the hoe. Big Jim examined his hands laughing. "First time I saw these soil busters they looked like you never did a day of honest work in your life."

"That's true," Berl replied welcoming the interruption.

"Look at them now," Big Jim said. "Look like the hands of a Mississippi Field hand. A no-account stoop laborer's hands. What did you do with them before?"

"I was a musician."

"What kind of musician?"

"A violinist. I played the violin."

"A Fiddler?"

"Yes."

"Well I'll be damned," Big Jim replied. "A red hot Fiddler?"

"Sometimes."

"You know Turkey in the Straw?"

"Yes."

"Maybe you'll play it for us, sometimes?"

"Yes."

"Funny thing about hands," Big Jim philosophized speaking slowly, thoughtfully. "There's two kinds of people in this world. Those working with their hands and those who don't and I favor those who know what it's like working with their hands. We live or die by our hands. The most

173

sacred part of our bodies. We find ourselves through our hands. That's how we know Redemption."

"Redemption? What is Redemption?" Berl asked.

Big Jim thought for a moment searching for words.

"Redemption is when you ask God for something and you don't get what you want but get something else. I asked for strength and got weakness that I might learn humbly to obey. I asked for health and got sickness. I asked for wealth and got poverty that I might be wise. I received nothing I asked for but everything I hoped for."

"And what is that?" Berl asked, struggling to understand.

"Longevity! Life! Despite myself, my prayers were answered. I am among all men most richly blessed!"

Through the years in prison as his friendship with Big Jim deepened Berl matured, influenced by someone who led a life of service to others. Big Jim explained: "You ain't much if you only live for yourself. You ain't much of a man if you don't serve some purpose greater than yourself."

"And what is your purpose?"

Big Jim laughed, waved his arm, pointing to the convicts crowding the Prison yard.

"You might say my purpose is to keep San Quentin from exploding. From blowing sky high! There's enough anger, frustration, hate and fear inside these walls that one day could leave nothing but bones and stones. Bones and stones. That's why you see me preaching trying to keep the peace between gangs of murderers and rapists. I'm the man in the middle of all this fury. The man in the middle. The Peacekeeper. I know how to talk to the hard-assess always looking for a fight." Big Jim turned to Berl and reaching out grasped his arm. A friendly gesture. "And you might also say my purpose is to save your lily-white ass. To keep you alive. Around here you are nothing but a piece of white meat. I tell you half the prison are sex offenders. Queers. Rapists. Child molesters. You name it we got it. Without knowing what to look out for you'd never live to do your time. Being a good looking white Jew Boy in San Quentin can kill you!"

"I thank you for that, Jim" Berl said gratefully. "I can never thank you enough."

"Now you don't want to blame the Cons for what they become here. It's dog eat dog, survival of the fittest. They come here young and angry and before leaving they are brutalized by the system and they survive by joining gangs fighting each other over which corner of the yard is their Turf. Most Cons never had a chance for a better life. They had no Daddy teaching them right from wrong. No real family. Mommy working her ass off, or selling her ass to pay the rent, put food on the table. And in the street they learn how to survive by being the toughest, meanest, most fearless bad-ass on the block. My preaching brotherly love don't make much difference. They're going where they're going and only a forgiving God can save them from the mean barren lives they've been given. I cry for them. They break my heart. But that don't do no good. That's why I'm always singing Hymns. Kind of eases the pain, don't you know."

The Prodigy

I must have a better purpose, Berl thought as he walked around the exercise yard thinking about what Big Jim had said. What is my purpose he wondered? He had been given so much in his previous life. His years and tears defined him as a man who someday looks back with regret knowing he once had the strength for everything and never used that strength. Returning to his cell he lay down on his bed and closed his eyes seeing himself as an old man, grey haired, bent over, his face wet with tears.

Thanks to Sergeant Emiliano Dante's diligence New York's Missing Persons Bureau had an outstanding record for finding truant children, Amnesia and Dementia patients, dead-beat debtors, blacked-out alcoholics and despairing souls contemplating suicide. Sergeant Dante was proud of this remarkable achievement with every unsolved case a personal affront. He transmitted wire photos to every Police department in the nation displaying Berl's photographs on Post Office walls in cities towns and villages in 48 states. When desperate for information, even standing on his head did not produce leads to Berl's disappearance. Exhausted by his search, hating failure, Sergeant Dante tried to escape his frustration in Broadway's Paramount Theater seeing "The All American Boy". Yes indeed, God does have a gift for the ironic. A love for fortune's startling reversals. Sergeant Dante didn't know whether to laugh or cry when after a long and disappointing search he finally found Berl up there on the silver screen. More mature, almost adult, no longer adolescent, Berl was now a handsome young man playing at being an inspiration to the youth of America. For years Sergeant Dante watched the rise and fall of Berl's career as avidly as any teen-age fan. He saw all his movies, read about his paternity and murder trials feeling outraged by a flagrant miscarriage of Justice. However He did succeed in establishing Menahim's mother's responsibility for Berl's broken arm enabling her son to win an international violin competition. Small satisfaction that did not relieve Sergeant Dante's despair. He applied for, and was granted permission to visit Berl in prison. A meeting Sergeant Dante hoped would enable him to write the final page of Berl's Dossier. The last paragraph or observation bringing closure to what had become Sergeant Dante's shameful obsession.

San Quentin's "Hall of Tears", a large high ceilinged chamber overlooking San Francisco Bay had slanting rays of sunlight shining through colored glass windows to lighten the room. Fog horns and crying seagulls outside the walls accompanied the subdued voices of prisoners and visiting families echoing their unhappiness. There was no laughter. A contagion of grief seemed to fill the air they breathed. Forbidden to embrace or kiss, husbands and wives, parents and children reached out across a wire barrier to touch each other with smiles and endearing words.

"I'm from New York City's Missing Persons Bureau," Sergeant Dante said introducing himself. "I had one hell of a time looking for you."

"I didn't know anyone was searching for me," Berl replied, surprised by the unexpected visitor.

The Prodigy

"You left no foot prints, nothing to go on. Not a clue," Dante complained.

"Maybe that's because I was on roller skates," Berl explained, smiling.

"Yes, that's possible," Sergeant Dante replied laughing. "We had no idea what you were doing or where you were going."

A loudspeaker on the wall announced the time remaining for this visiting session. Sergeant Dante looked at his watch and nodded.

"Why are you here?" Berl asked. "Why did you want to see me?"

Sergeant Dante hesitated, uncomfortable talking through a wire barrier to someone he could hardly see. Berl's face was indistinct. Without emotion. "Well, after years searching for you I felt we had to meet and maybe I could help with your appeal."

"There will be no appeal. No chance the verdict will be overturned," Berl insisted. "The Jury was no aberration. No exception. Finding innocent men guilty is as common as apple pie here in America the beautiful, home of the Brave."

"Not always," Sergeant Dante insisted.

In an adjacent booth visitors began sobbing. Berl and Dante waited for the crying to end. They silently stared at each other. Dante nodded sympathetically.

"I know you didn't kill Sylvia."

"True. But do you believe anyone cares about the truth?"

"Only the truth can make you free," Dante insisted. "Without regard for Truth our country has no future. We'll turn to dust."

"That's right," Berl said. "Dust and bones. We'll become a wasteland. A barren desert when the Rule of law is a joke only fools believe in."

"And what do you believe in?" Sergeant Dante asked.

"The Ten Commandments. The Golden Rule. Everything the All American Boy represented."

"Then you really believed in the role you were playing?"

"Not always," Berl replied. "When I first became Bobby Benson I thought he was too good to be true. Unbelievable. Unreal. But when I looked around and saw what was going on in this country I realized there was no other way to live. No other choice. The All American Boy was the best possible role for me to play."

"Why do you say that?" Dante asked.

"Because I'm from Brooklyn," Sergeant Dante. "I'm just a nice little boy from Brooklyn. You know, with all that has happened to me, I'm still Yidel mit de Fiddle. Yiddle mit de Fiddle."

"We will never go to the prison," replied Riva, Berl's mother to Sergeant Dante's call. Jacob, his father, listening in on the other phone added: "We have better things to do with our time than go and see what has become of our Berl." Sergeant Dante refused to accept No for an answer.

"You should visit him," Dante insisted. "I know what we will be looking at," Jacob shouted. "A Convict."

"For years Sergeant Dante," Riva added, "You have failed to find our boy raising our hopes with false leads. Such disappointment is painful. Cruel."

The Prodigy

"We've said Kaddish for our boy," Jacob said mournfully. "We've sat Shiva. The book of his life is closed forever."

"Then open it!" Sergeant Dante replied.

"My Berl was once a great and sensitive Artist, Sergeant Dante," Riva said shaking her head as she spoke into the phone. "A great and sensitive artist," she repeated mournfully. "I can't believe he would sink so low as to murder such a nice girl." Jacob raising his hand to his face nodded agreement, wiping away tears. "The good die young," Riva continued. "That's a fact of life. I will thank you to leave us to our sorrow. Our beautiful memories of what might have been, of the life Berl would have lived, had he lived the life we planned for him."

Governor Sam Sutter descended from the 49'ers who came to California during the Gold Rush to found a great state where impossible dreams came true. Seeking gold, they discovered a greater kind of wealth in a fabulous city on San Francisco Bay. Californians built three hundred mile Aqueducts diverting water from the High Sierra mountains to parched infertile deserts that became America's "Salad Bowl." Neither Earthquakes or Insurrections aborted the state's growth to prosperity while Governor Sam Sutter believed in the possibilities of the future.

The Governor was a restless man, working at a standup desk, pacing around his office, pausing to stare out the window as he dictated press releases, answered mail and composed messages to the State Legislature. The Press called him "Whirlwind Sam", a politician in constant motion like the wind-driven tumbling tumble weed blowing into the state from the Nevada desert.

State Police Chief Roy Emerson enjoyed working for the Governor. His Situation Reports were received with short direct questions. Law enforcement was uncorrupted by politics. His authority to maintain Law and order was respected by a hands-on Executive eager to know everything about the state he governed.

A worried Police Chief Emerson walked into the Governor's office with several Telex messages and waited for Sam Sutter to finish a phone call. Holding the receiver under one ear Sutter reached out for the messages glancing at them as he talked. Worried. Shaking his head, he put down the phone and asked: "What the hell is this Roy?"

"Trouble."

"Where?"

"San Quentin. Level two."

"Bad?"

"Could be."

"What has happened? The Governor asked.

"A couple of hard asses attacked a Guard. Beat him up bad."

"Why?"

"Seems like he's been over-using his baton. Cracked a few skulls. And now the prisoners won't come out into the yard for Roll Call."

"How many?"

"About a thousand."

"And in Level One?"

"No problem."

Governor Sutter read the Telex messages again. Frowning. "What do you want me to do?" he asked.

"There's nothing we can do until they cool down. Don't over react."

"For how long?"

"For as long as it takes. I've been talking with Big Jim, the Preacher. He's trying to hold back the crazies. So far they're listening to him."

"So what's next?"

"Keep talking. They got some Jail house lawyers calling themselves the Prison Rights Movement making demands we must meet before they calm down."

The Governor rose from behind his desk and walked to the window looking out over the State capitol at the distant snow-capped high Sierra mountains. "I'll give you twenty four hours."

"I'll need more Governor. They got a long list of what they're asking for."

"Like what?"

"Better living conditions. Better food, more visitation rights and amnesty for beating up the Guard." Governor Sutter threw the Telex messages down on his desk shouting "No way! No amnesty. They broke the law!"

"Then we must keep talking." Staring out the window, then turning to face Emerson, the governor hesitated a moment before replying: "If there's going to be a blood bath let's have it now!"

Berl had never witnessed unrestrained hatred. Looking out his cell window at the Level two high security compound he could not understand what was happening inside the barbed wire fence. Burning mattresses, smashing light bulbs, setting fire to the Prison Chapel, taking hostages, the rebelling prisoners were possessed by animal rage and fury. Violence was their language. Hatred their message. Berl turned to Big Jim and asked why?

"Beat an animal hard enough, long enough and they either fight back or lay down and die," Big Jim explained. "Same with human beings who never know a day in their life when they're not being beaten or humiliated to show them their place in this world. And that place ain't no good for man or boy trying to live with pride or dignity. They got no future but prison. Prison becomes their home and destination. Crime is how they get there."

"They can't all be bad," Berl asked. Big Jim nodded. "They would be good and decent if they had a chance to live that way. But that's not the way it is and that's not the way it's gonna be as long as Whitey does the fiddling with every threat to a Con's life making him angry. The hot flame of hatred burns more fiercely and every day he manages to stay alive is a triumph. After he survived the shit a couple of times he becomes more defiant!"

Chief Emerson walked into the Governor's office not waiting to be announced shouting: "They're going to execute Hostages tomorrow if we don't agree to their demands."

"How many Hostages?"

"Four."

Roy Emerson showed the Governor several photographs. "The Guards are held in the Yard. Hog tied, blindfolded, paraded around the yard for the newsreel cameras. The Press are interviewing their spokesman."

The Prodigy

Governor Sutton looked at a photograph and asked: "Who's that standing with the Hostages?"

"Big Jim the Preacher. He's saving them from having their throats cut. Singing Hymns and arguing with any of the hot-heads who would listen to reason."

"Where do we go from here?"

"Not into Hell, Governor. I hope, not into Hell!"

So this is the way the world ends, Berl said aloud, unable to sleep, listening to the agonized shouting of caged human beings in the yard below his cell window. He recalled reading: "the world ends not with a bang but a whimper" and at night he imagined he heard distressed souls whimpering in their sleep. Sobbing. Crying out in pain. This is the way the world ends Berl said to himself no matter what Big Jim with his hymns and prayers and hopes for mankind believed. "Go home and tell your neighbor," Big Jim sang. "Go home and tell your neighbor he died to save us all." Well how many more must die before salvation? Berl asked. A better world is a dream for Poets and Saints. There will be no respite from perpetual horror.

"God damn the Press driving me up the wall!" shouted Governor Sam Sutter. "A fucking circus with angry crowds screaming outside my home calling me the do nothing Governor! A spineless Wimp. A Leader who refuses to Lead! What the hell do they want me to do?" Police Chief Emerson waited for the Governor to finish his anguished cry. "Keep talking," he insisted. "Sooner or later the prisoners will give in. They haven't eaten or had a shower in three days. When they're hungry and filthy and tired of living in their own crap they'll surrender."

"Tomorrow's the fourth day."

"Yes."

"Four days tolerating lawlessness threatening the foundation of our civil society. Four days allowing murders and rapists to violate the Rule of law, the only power that keeps us from descending into barbarism. Into chaos! I have no choice Roy. No choice at all!"

"I don't agree Governor. Wait and talk, time is working for us. They have no food or water and with tonight's storm they'll be cold and wet."

Governor Sam Sutter returned to his desk, sat down and began writing a press statement. "This is for immediate release, Roy. Starting tomorrow noon I'll give them six hours to return to their cells.

"And then what?" asked Police Chief Emerson.

"You know what to do, Roy. I don't have to tell you how to enforce the Laws of the great state of California!"

Judge Sylvester Landau passionately believed in the Majesty of the Law, the Keystone supporting the arc of moral justice sustaining a civil society. Without the Rule of Law anarchy would prevail and savages stalk our streets. Judge Landau loathed the shyster lawyers extorting Movie Studios anxious to settle and avoid embarrassing publicity; he had contempt for ambitious Prosecutors litigating their way to the Governor's mansion. Corrupting the Law was indeed the greatest of all sins and highly publicized "Show Trials" tested his judicial patience. As a "hard-assed" Judge he presided without fear or favor, dispensing what he believed was -- "Equal Justice under Law".

Judge Landau recalled the newsreel cameras' hot lights and crowds of spectators overwhelming his courtroom's air conditioning. Angry objections and frequent interruptions evoked approval or dismay from a raucous audience refusing to remain silent. Judge Landau pounded the gavel calling for order threatening to clear the courtroom of spectators confident Berl's trial will go on despite their unruly behavior.

One spectator stood out from the crowd. A gray-haired old gentleman with a weather-lined face tanned by years at sea where wind salt air and sun indelibly marked a commercial Fisherman. Several days after giving his verdict, he saw the man again in his office waiting room. Judge Landau entered his private chambers, sat behind his desk, pressed the intercom and questioned the receptionist. Looking at his watch he said "I'll give him fifteen minutes." Turning to the door he watched the old man enter, hat in hand bowing respectfully.

"Thank you for seeing me your Honor." Judge Landau nodded, pointed at a chair. "Please sit down," he replied. "My secretary says you have something important to say to me."

"Yes, Your Honor."

"I believe you're the one spectator who never missed a day of the trial."

"Yes, your Honor."

"A Judicial Circus. A media frenzy. But you were well behaved."

"Yes, your Honor."

"Why are you here? Captain Angelo leaned forward in his chair and held out a bundle of letters. "I want you to read my daughter's letters."

"Your daughter?" Judge Landau said. Surprised.

"Yes, your Honor. I'm Sylvia's father. Read what she wrote and you will know the Jury made a mistake convicting an innocent man. A good man."

"The Jury has spoken," Judge Landau explained in his judicial voice. "A unanimous verdict."

Captain Angelo placed the letters on the table separating them. Pleading. "Read what Sylvia wrote and you will know the Jury did a great injustice."

Judge Landau picked up the letters and studied them for a moment. Shaking his head. Asking "Who else has read these letters?"

"Only the Prosecutor."

"And what did he do with them?"

"Nothing Your Honor."

"The Jury never saw them."

"Are you certain of that?"

"Yes, your Honor. The Prosecutor refused to take them from me."

Judge Landau picked up the letters holding them in his hand for a moment and without hesitating placed them in a desk drawer. Then, nodding at Captain Angelo, he said decisively: "I would like to read your daughter's letters Captain. Thank you for showing them to me."

Except at the State Fair's Shooting Gallery Berl had never heard gunfire. Listening to two uninterrupted minutes of shooting following the explosion of stun bombs and tear gas grenades, he could not imagine anyone deliberately firing live ammunition into a Prison yard crowded with human beings. Journalist describing the slaughter said this moment in our nation's shameful history "was like shooting fish in a barrel".

The next morning Berl looked down at the Prison Yard and watched the Medics searching through a mass of bodies looking for survivors. He heard their excited cries when discovering a sign of life. A flickering eye lid. An agonized moan. A call for help. The Prison Guards grabbed the corpses by their legs and dragged them to the morgue leaving behind on the pavement trails of blood that could not be completely washed away with high pressure fire hoses.

He looked for Big Jim to explain what happened. Big Jim would help him understand this tragedy. But the Preacher was no more. Hopefully gone to his reward in the heavens he so passionately believed in.

Berl could never again look out his cell window. Or in his mind's eye, not see bodies scattered across the Prison yard like broken dolls. Every day at noon when the Power Plant's steam whistle announced the time, he heard what sounded like human cries for mercy. He could not read. His favorite books refused to come alive. He found no refuge in sleep. Closing cell doors shattered his composure. He felt like a hollowed out tree struck by lightning. A walking dead man living a burned-out existence feeling the dread, fatigue, tension, pains, tics, stammers and impatience with frustration that accompanied a nervous breakdown. He did not enjoy working at the Prison farm where he had long conversations with someone who existed only in his troubled mind. He lived from day to day with no companion but the persistent voice in his head he struggled to answer.

"I am the Balm of Gilead," the voice said, "come to heal your wounded soul."

"Who are you?" Berl demanded startled by the intrusion. "Who am I talking to?"

"Do not stand at my grave and cry," the voice commanded. "I am Big Jim! I did not die!"

"You did die!" Berl insisted. "I saw your body dragged across the yard to the morgue."

"Yes! My body!" the voice replied. "But not my soul." To silence the voice, Berl furiously chopped into the soil with a hoe as if to inter the disturbing apparition. "You cannot be!" he shouted. "I saw you dead and buried!"

"I'm here to help you," the voice said. " I am your Dybbuk!"

"Dybbuk" Berl asked. "What is a Dybbuk?"

"A wandering soul come to help you rejoin with God! A man must live more than one life before that happens."

"I don't believe in God!" Berl shouted. "There is no God!"

"God is love!"

"God is a fantasy. A word without meaning."

"All words have meaning. Words are the mysterious passers-by of the soul! And they that wait upon the Lord and hear his word shall renew their strength. They shall mount up with wings as eagles; they shall run and not be weary, and they shall walk, and not faint. The truth is that we are not alone, all of us together create God."

The Prodigy

Berl stopped eating, not rising from his bed after sleepless nights. He lost weight, his hair turned grey, and chronically depressed, he lost interest in living. Dr. Francis Feelgood, director of San Quentin's mental health facility placed Berl on a "Suicide Watch" employing aggressive therapies dating back to the dark ages of medicine. Seated for hours in a tub of ice water, his head protruding through a hole in the black rubber cover, Berl cooled down to a core temperature believed low enough to cure depression. Then standing in a shower, high-pressure hoses alternately warmed and chilled his body attempting to raise his melancholy spirits. Learning he was scheduled for electroconvulsive shock treatments Berl refused to be strapped onto a Gurney with his arms and legs restrained, a rubber protector in his mouth, a band of electrodes around his skull as Dr. Feelgood poured lightning into his brain.

Escaping the hospital's minimum security area should be easy, Berl thought, watching civilian employees arrive every morning at nine, and at five take a Bus to their homes in nearby San Quentin village. At the Main gate Guards routinely allowed the Bus to pass unexamined. In a Staff locker room Berl stole and put on a hospital worker's blue "Scrubs" and unchallenged, boarded the evening bus to freedom. Travelling past shopping Malls, homes, schools, and churches Berl thought about the people living out their lives in those homes enjoying the freedom to think and speak their own thoughts, have their own dreams, living whatever life they wished. As an escaped convict he was still a prisoner. "Aren't we all prisoners?" He asked himself. "Like the convicts in San Quentin and those who guard them? Can anyone be truly free?"

Standing on the side of the coastal highway Berl raised his thumb for a ride to downtown San Francisco and the Fisherman's Wharf where Fishing boats moored between voyages harvesting the sea of tuna, sardines, salmon and albacore. He arrived on the day of the annual Blessing of the Fleet and watched the fishing boats parade past a Priest who raised his hand making the sign of the Cross asking God's protection from the perils of the sea. The boats were named after Saints, wives, mothers, Fathers, and Children. Berl looked for one name forever imprinted on his soul. He fantasized about finding a boat named Sylvia and going to sea with Captain Angelo finding sanctuary in Alaska's stormy waters. When he found Captain Angelo he was disappointed.

"You are now a criminal," Captain Angelo insisted. "I will not be your accomplice. Helping you escape is a Felony. I could lose my boat."

Berl insisted. Pleaded. Captain Angelo was adamant. "The only place I'll take you is San Quentin."

When they arrived at the Prison hospital Dr. Feelgood welcomed them, waving a telegram. "It seems," Dr. Feelgood said reluctantly, "I'm going to lose my most promising patient just when we were about to succeed with your treatment." He handed the telegram to Berl. "This is a Court Order for your immediate release," Dr. Feelgood explained. "The Judge dismissed the Jury's verdict. The Prosecutor withheld exculpatory evidence. Your conviction is null and void." Berl read the telegram struggling to understand. "You are free to go and resume your life," Dr. Feelgood said confidently, "Where I assure you, your future has infinite possibilities of renewal."

Berl returned to Brooklyn to stand under the stairs of a subway station where the tracks ran elevated above the street. A street musician playing the violin for nickels, dimes and quarters dropped into the case at his feet. Winter or summer, rain or shine he performed for commuters who stopped to hear him. He also played in apartment courtyards where housewives leaned out of their windows to applaud and throw down coins as he played with great passion and beauty -- "None but the Lonely heart can know my anguish. I'm alone, -- and far apart, -- from joy and gladness."

Returning to his apartment, Sergeant Dante played his favorite recordings, soul-stirring music banishing his disappointment pursuing the Bureau's elusive quarry. Closing his eyes, leaning back in a comfortable armchair, he accompanied the Librettos imagining himself singing, bowing and raising his arms to acknowledge the audience's appreciative applause. "A little make-believe is good for the soul," his father once said, and Sergeant Dante agreed. A little make-believe is an improvement on reality. When he learned of Berl now living as a street musician, Sergeant Dante rose from his armchair and walked across the room and opened a window. Raising his arms to the heavens as if to thank a benign God he sang, accompanied by the golden voice of Enrico Caruso, Paglacci's final Aria crying out in an exultant voice: "La Commedia e Finita! La Commedia e Finita!"

About the Author

After a fifty year career as writer, director and producer of many award winning films and television programs, Norman Weissman has written four Novels and a Memoir. Determined to oppose the silence in which lies become history the author fulfills his obligation to all who have told him their stories. He lives in Connecticut with his wife Eveline.

Also by Norman Weissman

Acceptable Losses A Novel
Snapshots USA A Novel
Oh Palestine A Novel
My Exuberant Voyage A Memoir